THE SEC

John Fardell works a
designer and occasional ~~~~ ~~~~ ~~~~ ~~~~ ~~utor
to *Viz* (he is the creator of 'The Modern Parents' and 'The
Critics' amongst others), hi~~~~ ~~~~ ~~~~ ~~~~ ~~~~
Independent, the *List*, the *H*~~~~ ~~~~
Evening Standard. He is ma~~~~ ~~~~
Edinburgh. *The Secret of the* ~~~~
book for Faber, and follow~~~~ ~~~~ ~~~~ ~~~~ ~~~~h
and *The Flight of the Silver Turtle*. John is also the author and
illustrator of a children's picture book, *Manfred the Baddie*.

D0526247

The SECRET of the BLACK MOON MOTH

John Fardell

ff

faber and faber

First published in 2009
by Faber and Faber Limited
Bloomsbury House, 74–77 Great Russell Street, WC1B 3DA

Typeset by Faber and Faber Limited
Printed in the UK by CPI Bookmarque, Croydon

A CIP record for this book
is available from the British Library

ISBN 978-0-571-22692-4

10 9 8 7 6 5 4 3 2 1

To Catherine, Peter and Alice,
with love

Prologue

Port of Genoa, Italy

The man crawled across the moonlit roof towards the boarded-up skylight, his face concealed by a black balaclava. He reached the skylight and, working as quietly as possible, prised it open using a short metal crowbar. He looked down into the space beneath him, but could make out nothing. Could this really be the place – the home of the man he had followed earlier? Could anyone really be living up here in the loft of this old warehouse? Or had his precarious climb up the rusting iron ladder and crumbling brickwork been a waste of time?

After checking there were no sounds of breathing or snoring below, the man took a slim black torch from his jacket, and sent a narrow beam of light down into the loft room, scanning what was there. A wooden table. A few chairs. A threadbare rug on unvarnished floorboards. He spotted a newspaper lying open on the table. A recent newspaper.

Someone *was* living here. This was the right place.

He lowered himself through the skylight until his feet reached the table. From there, it was easy to clamber down to the floor. The table creaked slightly, and the man glanced nervously towards the closed door at the far end of the room. He had no way of knowing where the inhabitant of this loft apartment had his bedroom, but it could be just next door.

Fortunately, this looked like the room he wanted. The two side walls were lined with bookshelves, and a book was what he was looking for. Systematically, he swept his torch beam along each shelf, checking every spine. There were hundreds of books: books in Italian, books in English, books in dozens of other languages.

The book he was seeking was old. Most of the books on the shelves were old, but he couldn't spot anything that looked like the one he was after. Damn!

A thought occurred to him. The book had only recently been purchased. Would its new owner have shelved it away already? Surely it was more likely that he would still be reading it and studying it. In which case, he might well have put it beside his bed.

The man started creeping towards the door. He had hoped to avoid any contact with the book's owner, and he would avoid waking him if possible. But he was determined to get what he had come for.

Just before he reached the door, something in the corner of the room caught his eye. A small writing desk. Worth checking out first. He went over to it and tried to open its sloping top. It was locked, but his crowbar soon solved that problem, opening it with a dull crack and the crunch of splintering wood. The man glanced at the door, but heard no one stirring.

He shone his torch down into the desk. There! A slim vol-

4

ume with an age-cracked brown leather cover. No writing on the front, just a strange design, hand-drawn in black ink – a silhouette of some sort of tropical butterfly or moth. He opened the book. Pages of faded inked handwriting, elaborately styled and all in some sort of  cipher, written on ancient yellowed and mottled paper. Result! This had to be it.

Suddenly, the door began to creak open. The man instantly switched off his torch and pocketed it, at the same time grabbing the book. He rushed at the person entering the room, pulling a narrow flat object from his jacket pocket and pressing a button on it with his thumb. *Flick*. The object's slender blade sprang out from the front end and clicked into place. The man could just make out the form of the newcomer in the darkness of the room, and he lunged forward with his flick-knife. But the other person dodged and somehow managed to grasp one side of the book.

For a second or two, they had the book between them, stretched open with one holding the front half and one holding the back half, neither letting go. The owner of the book cried out. The man thrust with his knife again, this time managing to plunge it into the other's ribs, turning his cry into a deathly choking rasp.

The man's victim fell back, but his fingers still clung to the book. The man felt the antique leather spine tear apart, and heard the half-book hit the floor just after the body of the person he had stabbed.

Cursing, the man retracted his knife blade, swapped the weapon for his torch, and started to scan the floor. Damn! The pages had scattered everywhere. As he stepped over the body to get to them, he looked down and saw, in the torchlight, the face of his victim. And he gasped, startled by whom he saw.

Then, before he could start to gather the strewn pages, he heard footsteps pounding along floorboards from another part of the loft. Footsteps of more than one person. Too many to risk fighting, and getting nearer fast. Stuffing the half of the book he'd retained into his largest pocket, he jumped onto the table and sprang for the skylight.

Fifteen minutes later, after a recklessly speedy descent from the warehouse roof and a hell-for-leather sprint through the dockside alleyways, the man was back in one of the city's brightly lit tourist areas, ambling back to his hotel as if he were simply returning from a nightclub.

His mind was racing. If only he'd realised who was living there, realised whom he'd been following, he could have gone in better prepared. Could have saved himself a lot of trouble. But he couldn't have known.

There was nothing more he could do here in Genoa. He knew that the others who lived in the warehouse loft would be gone by the morning, along with the other half of the book and the body of his victim. He was sure that the stab wound he'd inflicted had been fatal, but he was equally sure that the killing would never be reported to the police. He was quite safe on that score.

And at least he'd got half of the book. Maybe it would be enough. It would have to be enough. He had a good feeling. And from now on, he would make sure he was fully prepared and fully equipped. He was on the trail now, and nothing was going to stop him.

'The world', declared Professor Garrulous Gadling, 'contains more mysteries than we can imagine.' He was standing behind an antique wooden lectern on the lecture hall stage of the Royal Westminster Institute of Natural History, an imposing historic building in Parlington Square, in the heart of London. He had just started giving an early evening talk, entitled 'Little-Known Animal Species of Our Planet'.

Professor Gadling was a pear-shaped man in his late sixties. His large beaky nose and double chin gave him a rather pelican-like appearance, an impression enhanced by the crumpled cream suit he was wearing. The outfit was embellished by a polka-dotted red bow tie and a matching handkerchief stuffed loosely into his top jacket pocket, and topped off with a well-travelled panama hat.

'Some people may think', he continued, 'that modern science has more or less pinned down all there is to know, but such a view would be piffle. Science is not about merely listing what we know, but about making a never-ending journey into what we *don't* know. And *that*, of course, is the fun of it.' He bestowed a wide-mouthed beam on his audience.

Sam Carnabie, an eleven-year-old boy sitting in the front row, grinned back. He'd been looking forward to this evening for ages – looking forward to Professor Gadling's lecture and, most of all, to being with the friends who were seated along the row to either side of him.

To Sam's right were a twelve-year-old girl called Zara, her eleven-year-old brother Ben, and a gangly man with a pink bald head fringed by wiry white hair – Professor Alexander Ampersand. Professor Ampersand, an inventor by profession, was Zara and Ben's great-uncle. He had adopted them as babies when their Tanzanian father and Scottish mother had been killed in a car crash. Sam's parents had once been students of Professor Ampersand, and had arranged for Sam to spend his last two school holidays at the Ampersands' amazing, invention-filled house in Edinburgh.

To Sam's left were a brown-haired thirteen-year-old girl called Marcia, and a woman in her sixties called Professor Petunia Hartleigh-Broadbeam. She was also an inventor, based in London, and had recently become Marcia's legal guardian. (Marcia's sophisticated, glamorous, but thoroughly repulsive parents were in prison.)

To the far side of Professor Hartleigh-Broadbeam sat a tall, sinewy man called Professor Eric Gauntraker. He was an explorer, and of a similar age to Professors Gadling, Ampersand and Hartleigh-Broadbeam; the four of them were all old friends and one-time colleagues.

In the short time that Sam had known Zara, Ben and Marcia they'd been through two extraordinary adventures together, and had become the best of friends. It had been a few weeks since they'd last seen one another, and Professor Gadling's lecture this Saturday evening in mid-September had provided the perfect opportunity for a get-together in London. Sam lived in Hertfordshire, and that afternoon he'd made the short train journey into King's Cross Station by himself, where he'd met Zara, Ben and Professor Ampersand off their train from Edinburgh. The plan was for everyone to go to a restaurant after the lecture, before going back to Marcia and Professor Hartleigh-Broadbeam's flat, where they were all staying for the weekend.

'In my own career as a naturalist and explorer,' continued Professor Gadling, 'I have specialised particularly in the study of unusual and little-known creatures, and I thought it might be entertaining to tell you about some of them this evening.'

Zara glanced round at the rest of the audience, which seemed to consist entirely of rather serious-looking adults, who she guessed must be members of the Institute. Zara knew that this was the first time Professor Gadling had been given the opportunity to deliver a lecture to this prestigious and influential organisation, and she knew how important it was to him that his talk went down well. So far, however, the members' faces seemed as unresponsive to Professor Gadling's breezy good humour as the stately stone architecture of the hall.

'I shall begin', said Professor Gadling, 'with the African hunting bat.' He switched on a slide projector, and, as the lights dimmed, a picture of a bat became visible on a screen at the back of the stage – not a photograph, but a pen-and-ink sketch on lined notepaper.

'Like many bats,' continued Professor Gadling, 'the African hunting bat is small; but *unlike* other bats, it hunts creatures that are a great many times its own size. It does this by working collectively. African hunting bats live in vast colonies. As night falls, the bats leave their roosting cave together and fly low across the savannah, sweeping the ground with their high-pitched sonar waves. As soon as one of the bats detects a potential prey – typically a sleeping wildebeest – it signals to the others, and the whole group closes in. The wildebeest may be startled by the wing-beats and begin to run, but to no avail. Using sophisticated vocal signals and highly skilled formation flying, the bats box in the fleeing animal. Then, as one, they strike. Several thousand tiny flying bats sink their teeth into every part of the wildebeest's body, lift it forty feet into the air, then drop it, killing it instantly. Then the bats swarm onto the carcass and devour it with the ferocity of piranha fish, stripping it to the bare bones within minutes.'

'Professor Gadling!' A dry, displeased voice interrupted Professor Gadling's flow. The children turned to see the speaker, a waspish-looking man who had risen to his feet at one end of the front row.

'Professor Gadling,' he said, 'as president of the Institute, I must inform you that this establishment is dedicated to the serious study of the biological sciences. We assumed that you wished to present us with factual research into genuine species, not ludicrous tales of non-existent creatures. Perhaps you thought it acceptable to begin your lecture with a piece of fanciful nonsense in order to amuse these children' – he looked along the front row disapprovingly – 'who I assume are acquaintances of yours, but I must ask you to restrict yourself to subject matter suitable for an educated adult audience.'

'*Fanciful nonsense?*' cried Professor Gadling, indignantly. 'I assure you that I would never dream of patronising *anyone* with fanciful nonsense, children or adults. If these young people *are* more entertained by my lecture than you are, it is because they possess an open-mindedness that you clearly lack.'

'There is a difference between open-mindedness and credulity!' retorted the president. 'You surely can't be expecting a room full of world-renowned experts such as us to believe that this—this African hunting bat actually exists?'

'Of course it exists!' insisted Professor Gadling. 'As do all the creatures that I am planning to talk about this evening: the great Alaskan snow toad, the parasitic puffer sprat, the sand-snorkelling shrew of the Western Sahara, to name but a few. Just because an animal has yet to be officially recorded and catalogued by Western scientists doesn't mean it doesn't exist. There are dozens of species whose existence is now beyond dispute – the electric eel, the duckbilled platypus, the giant squid – that were once dismissed as "travellers' tales" or "native myths" by the self-appointed experts of the time. Now, if I may be allowed to return to the subject of the African hunting bat—'

'Enough!' snapped the president. He turned to the audience. 'I declare this fiasco of a lecture terminated. I am sorry that we have all had our evening wasted. I *knew* it was a mistake to start allowing non-members to give talks to the Institute. Well, never again!' Putting on his overcoat, he strode towards the doors at the back of the hall. Tuts, mutters and the scraping of chair legs on marble echoed around the hall as the collected members of the Royal

Westminster Institute of Natural History rose to their feet and followed him.

2

'Wait!' yelled Zara crossly, standing up. 'Don't all leave just because *he* told you to!'

'Yeah, come back!' shouted Ben.

'You'll miss a really good lecture!' called Sam.

'You might *learn* something!' added Marcia.

'It's no use,' said Professor Gadling, gathering up his notes and his slides. 'Let them go. I was clearly wasting my breath on them, and there's no sense in you wasting yours too. Thank you, though,' he added, stepping down from the stage.

'I'm really sorry, Garrulous,' said Professor Ampersand, patting his friend's arm sympathetically.

'Ignoramuses!' snorted Professor Hartleigh-Broadbeam, casting a ferocious glare at the river of people flowing from the hall. 'If I'd thought it would have done any good, I'd have blocked the exit and whacked 'em all back into their seats.' She was a large and striking woman who looked quite capable of carrying out both tasks.

'Well,' said Professor Gadling, 'I suppose I can forget any hopes I had that the Royal Westminster Institute of Natural History might sponsor my planned expedition to research the voice-throwing marmoset of Costa Rica.'

'You're better off without the help of an institute like this,' growled Professor Gauntraker. 'Narrow-minded pen-pushers. I'd like to see how they'd manage in the middle of the Kalahari with night closing in and only a broken pocket-knife for survival; then they'd see how much good their precious book-learning is.'

Zara could recall one or two occasions in the past when Professor Gauntraker had himself accused Professor Gadling of inventing the species he talked about. But this evening, loyalty toward his old colleague clearly took precedence over any such doubts.

'Anyway,' said Professor Gadling, putting his notes away into an old leather shoulder bag, 'let us dwell on these unenlightened people no further. How are you all? I didn't get a chance to talk to you before my lecture. Is your electric plane and vehicle business going well?'

Professor Ampersand had recently invented a powerful new type of electric motor, and he and Professor Hartleigh-Broadbeam had gone into partnership with a young aircraft designer called Amy McAirdrie, who lived and worked in a dilapidated old hangar on a beach near Edinburgh. Over the summer, the two professors and the four children had helped Amy to build an electric-powered plane – a small amphibious flying boat called the *Silver Turtle*. The project had led the children into a perilous struggle against a dangerous international organisation, but all had ended well, with the little plane proving to be a remarkably successful aircraft. The conclusion of these events had been reported in the media, and the publicity had begun to attract some much-needed financial backing for the fledgling electric aircraft and vehicle company.

'The business is going OK,' Professor Ampersand told Professor Gadling, 'though it's early days.'

'It's still a struggle to convince some people that non-polluting electric cars and planes are both viable and nec-

14

essary,' remarked Professor Hartleigh-Broadbeam.

'Yeah,' said Marcia, 'you'd think it would be really obvious to *everyone* how urgent it is that we stop using carbon-based fuels, but people are so *stupid*.' Marcia had become increasingly concerned about environmental issues recently – pollution, habitat destruction, species extinction, global warming. It made her angry the way humans were wrecking the planet, endangering not just their own survival but that of all living species.

'Not *all* people are stupid,' Ben pointed out. 'A lot of people have been really interested in Uncle Alexander's motors, and in Amy's plane designs.'

'That's good to hear,' said Professor Gadling. 'And how is Amy?'

'She's fine,' said Zara. 'She had a cousin's wedding to go to in Glasgow this weekend; otherwise she'd have flown us all down in the *Silver Turtle*. She sends her apologies for missing your lecture.'

'Well, she didn't miss much,' said Professor Gadling, smiling ruefully. 'Come on; let's go and have some supper. I know an excellent but cheap Italian place near here.'

'Lead us to it,' said Professor Hartleigh-Broadbeam. 'We've clearly more than outstayed our welcome here.' The last of the audience members had trickled through the exit, and a frowning uniformed official was now standing by the doors, jangling his keys pointedly.

Soon, the four children and four professors were outside and making their way down the Institute's wide front steps. The air was warm for mid-September and the sky was just turning dark, a deepening blue backdrop to the many floodlit buildings they could see around Parlington Square and beyond. 'Now then,' said Professor Gadling, 'the restaurant is just a couple of streets away, near—'

 'Er, 'scuse me, Professor Gadling.' A weak, hesitant voice, with a London accent, interrupted Professor Gadling's. They all turned to see a man following them down the steps. He must have been standing by the big stone pillars of the Institute's entrance, waiting for them to come out, Zara thought.

They paused at the foot of the steps to allow the stranger to catch up with them. He was a small man who looked to be in his early seventies, with a rather mournful face and stooped shoulders. His pale grey hair was cut short around the back and sides, with a few thin strands combed across the top in an unsuccessful attempt to cover his balding scalp. Beneath a shabby brown raincoat, he wore a tightly buttoned grey suit made from some thick ancient fabric that had gone shiny with wear and grime, a shirt that had lost any crispness or whiteness it may have once had, and a thin, badly knotted tie. An uncomfortable-looking strap across his shoulder and chest supported a bulky old leather satchel at his hip. 'I—I'm sorry to trouble you, professor,' he stuttered, shuffling his feet and twisting his hands together in front of him. 'But I wanted to say that I enjoyed your talk. Th—the bit you were able to give, I mean. I'm sorry it got cut short.' As soon as he had blurted out the words, he looked down at the pavement.

'Thank you!' said Professor Gadling. 'How very kind of you to wait around to say so.' He smiled ruefully. 'Sadly, most of your fellow members didn't seem to share your opinion, did they?'

'Fellow members?' echoed the man. 'Crumbs, no! *I'm* not a member of the Institute!' He sounded quite aston-ished that anyone could have imagined such a thing. 'I'm n—not even a real scientist or anything. And even if I was ... well, you saw for yourself what they're like.' He glanced up at the Institute's neoclassical façade with an expression that Zara thought was a strange mixture of awe and bitterness. 'No, I only came here tonight because I read in the paper that you were giving a lecture,' continued the man. 'I sneaked in and sat at the back where I wouldn't be noticed.' Zara wondered why he had felt it necessary to make himself so unobtrusive. The lecture had been advertised as a public event. This man seemed to have a very low opinion of himself. 'I–I've been wanting to meet you for a while, actually, professor,' he went on nervously. 'Since I read about you in the newspapers a few weeks ago. And I–I was hoping that you might also be able to introduce me to the other professors I read about: your friends with the small flying boat, and Professor Gauntraker the explorer. I've got something I want to show to you all.' He quietened his already soft voice to a whisper. 'Something that I promise you'll find totally extraordinary.'

He looked down at his hands again, with his head bowed and shoulders turned in, as if he was trying to shrink away to nothing from the embarrassment of having dared to spill out so many words.

'The other professors you mention are right here,' said Professor Gadling, gesturing. 'Actually we're about to go and have supper, so—'

'I'm sorry! I'm holding you up, aren't I?' said the man instantly. 'I'm really sorry for bothering you. It was stupid of me.' He turned and started to scurry away along the pavement.

'Wait!' called Professor Gadling. 'I was *about* to say, why don't you come and join us and show us these extraordinary things while we eat?'

The man stopped and looked back. 'Oh no,' he said, looking as if he could hardly believe that such an invitation had been offered. 'I couldn't. I couldn't gatecrash your evening like that.'

'Nonsense!' said Professor Gadling. 'You've aroused our curiosity. And we'd be glad of your company, wouldn't we?' he added, turning to the others.

'Oh absolutely! Please come,' said Professor Hartleigh-Broadbeam, and everyone quickly added their assurances that he must. Zara sensed that the adults were mainly inviting the man along out of kindness, rather than because they really expected to be shown anything extraordinary. But kindness was reason enough. They couldn't possibly let this painfully shy man just slink away, looking so lonely and miserable.

'Well, if you're really sure I'm not being a nuisance . . .' said the man, hovering hesitantly.

'Good man,' said Professor Gadling, shepherding the man into the group as they set off along the pavement. 'Now, let me introduce everyone properly.' He did so, and they all shook the man's hand in turn as they walked.

'I'm Wilfred,' he said. 'Wilfred Lugg.'

Professor Gadling led them along a series of narrow roads and side-lanes, keeping up a babble of small talk, tactfully making sure their shy new acquaintance felt included in the group without pressuring him to talk about himself.

The pavements were busy, giving this corner of the capital a vibrant atmosphere of early evening bustle. The air was rich with the smells of restaurant food, and the streets glowed with pub lanterns, illuminated shop signs, and the headlights of buses and taxis.

Ben liked London. The immense size and complexity of the place fascinated him. He remembered his great-uncle once remarking, on a previous visit, that London was a city where you might find anything or anyone from any corner of the world. The thought of such limitless possibilities had always given Ben a tingle of excitement down his spine, and he found himself experiencing that same tingling sensation now. In spite of Wilfred's awkward, unconfident manner, there had been *something* in his voice – or maybe in his eyes – that had left Ben with the feeling that perhaps this man *did* have something totally extraordinary to show them.

'Here we are,' said Professor Gadling, stopping in front of a small Italian restaurant.

The proprietor greeted Professor Gadling warmly and ushered them all to a secluded corner at the rear of the cosy, candlelit interior, where he slid three tables together. In no time at all, food had been ordered and drinks had arrived – lemonade for the children and wine for the adults, except Wilfred, who insisted he'd prefer water.

'Now then,' said Professor Gadling, 'let's have a look at this thing you want to show us, Wilfred. Is it some invention you've been working on, or a book you've been writing, perhaps?' he prompted, encouragingly.

'It's nothing like that,' said Wilfred. He hesitated for just a moment, then reached into his satchel, which he'd kept beside his chair, and brought out a large square biscuit tin. The tin looked several decades old. The lettering on its sides and lid was faded and scratched, and spelled out the name of a long-extinct brand.

Everyone leaned forward as Wilfred took off the lid and carefully lifted something out from a protective cocoon of crumpled tissue paper. 'That's what I wanted to show you,' he said, placing the object down on the table.

It was a human skull.

3

For several seconds, they all looked at the skull without saying anything. Something about it gave Zara an odd feeling inside, a feeling that was hard to define. A feeling of strangeness. *Otherness.* She sensed that this feeling was shared by everyone else, and she tried to pinpoint what it was about the skull that was so unsettling. Was it just that its darkly mottled grey-brown surface gave an impression of extreme age? Or was it merely the way it was bathed in the soft, slightly wavering candlelight of the restaurant? Or was there something more particularly strange about it? Although the skull's basic shape looked similar to that of other human skulls Zara had seen in books and films, the more she stared at it, the more she began to think that some of its features didn't look quite right in shape and size. And now she noticed two slightly raised ridges on the top of the skull, widely spaced and running from front to back.

'Fascinating!' said Professor Gadling, breaking the silence at last. 'Absolutely fascinating.' He carefully picked up the skull with both hands and studied it closely from all angles. 'Clearly the skull of *some* sort of human, yet not that of our own species, *Homo sapiens.* The eye sockets are too big and the lower face and jaw are too small,' he pointed out, clarifying what it was that had seemed out of proportion to Zara. 'And these two ridges along the cranium are quite unlike anything you'd find on a modern human skull,' he continued. 'This must be the skull of an earlier human species. One of our long-extinct evolutionary ancestors or cousins. But I don't know enough about the subject to be able to identify which one. Where was it found, Wilfred?' he said, putting the skull back on the table. 'And by whom?'

'By me,' said Wilfred, looking rather overcome, but pleased with the level of interest his skull had aroused. 'I found it back in 1954, on the island of Pulau Gigi Naga, in Southeast Asia. Pulau Gigi Naga is uninhabited and pretty small – only seven miles long and four miles across – so you might not've heard of it. It's in the South China Sea, about six hundred miles east of the Malay Peninsula and about three hundred miles north of Borneo. Very isolated.'

Ben hadn't heard of Pulau Gigi Naga, though he could picture the bit of sea that Wilfred meant. A map of Southeast Asia was one of the many maps that covered his bedroom walls and ceiling back home. 'Are you an explorer?' he asked Wilfred.

'Me?' said Wilfred. 'Oh no. I was a private in the army at the time I found this, doing my National Service – compulsory for all young men back then. My regiment was sent out to what was then the British colony of Malaya – part of what's now Malaysia, of course. Towards the end of my time out there, a small group of us were sent on an expedition to Pulau Gigi Naga, to make a rough survey of the island. I think the army wanted to check out the place for possible future uses – as a fuel depot for shipping, or a training site, or whatever. Anyway, we had to make our way through the tropical rainforest that covers most of the island and up into the group of hills in the centre of the island. The hills are topped by twelve tall, sharply pointed rocky crags, which are what gives the island its name. *Pulau* is the Malay word for island. *Gigi* means teeth, and *naga* means dragon.'

'Island of the Teeth of the Dragon,' said Ben. 'Cool!'

'Anyway,' continued Wilfred, 'our platoon travelled quite slowly, mapping the island's main features as we went. After two days, we reached a small lake, which we camped beside for the night. Early the next morning, while I was having a wash at the edge of the lake, I noticed a rock-face a little way into the forest, a couple of hundred yards away, and I thought I could see the opening to a cave. I went to have a look, and there was a cave all right, but I quickly found that it didn't go back very far. The back of the cave narrowed to a crevice, and this was blocked up by boulders and rubble which also covered most of the cave floor. It looked like there'd been a rockfall from the cave roof at some point in the past. I was about to leave when I spotted something sticking out from under some of the rubble on the floor. Something that looked like the bones of a hand.

'I started trying to shift the rubble off the bones. Some boulders were too heavy – I was never very strong, even back then – but I managed to clear enough of the smaller ones to uncover most of a human skeleton. It was crushed and broken in places, but looked just about complete. About six foot long, it was, so I could tell it had been an adult. I guessed that the person whose skeleton it was must have been killed by the rockfall. Maybe there'd been some kind of earthquake. I could see from its darkened colour that the skeleton was very old, but at first I just assumed it was that of an ordinary human. Then, when I looked more carefully, I wasn't so sure. Like you, I noticed how different the skull was, and the arms didn't look quite right either. They were slightly too long for the body – not as long as an orang-utan's or anything, but a bit longer than a person's. I remembered having read something in a magazine once about how scientists knew about earlier species of human from digging up their skeletons. I was always interested in science, even though I'd done badly at school. I began to wonder if I'd found such a skeleton.

'Then I noticed something else, lying among the stones beside the skeleton. What I'd spotted was this.' Wilfred took from the biscuit tin another tissue-paper-covered object, much smaller than the skull. He unwrapped it and put it on the table. The object was carved from some sort of black stone-like substance. It was almost flat, and its shape was almost triangular, though its three edges were curved not straight. One of its three corners extended into a long thin tendril with a flat, ragged end. The total length of the object, including the tendril, was about twelve centimetres, and its width between the other two corners about six centimetres. Its surface was shiny, as if polished, and engraved with a complex pattern of squiggly grooved lines.

'You can see it's been carved by someone,' said Wilfred, 'but I've never been able to work out what it is.'

'I think the type of stone it's carved from is jet, isn't it?' said Zara.

'I agree,' said Professor Ampersand. 'Though, strictly speaking, jet isn't a stone; it's fossilised organic matter, like amber or coal. As to what this *is*, I suppose it could have

23

been the blade of some sort of scraping tool.'

Professor Gauntraker picked the object up and held it close to his face. 'It looks more ornamental than practical to me,' he said. 'These lines look a little like the markings I've seen on the religious artefacts of certain tribal peoples I've lived amongst. Intriguing.'

'May I have a closer look, Eric?' said Professor Gadling, taking the object. He too peered at it closely, then traced a finger around its outline, nodding to himself as he did so. 'Well I can't say what this was *for*,' he said, 'but I *can* identify what it's a carving *of*. It's a remarkably accurate sculpture of the left-side wings of a particular species of moth: the Malaysian moon moth – *Actias maenas*, to give it its scientific name, and the male of the species, to be precise.'

'Goodness, that's very specific, Garrulous!' said Professor Hartleigh-Broadbeam. 'Are you sure?'

'Absolutely,' said Professor Gadling. 'I know the species well, and, believe me, the distinctive curved angles of the front wing and this long trailing part of the rear wing are quite unmistakable. This slightly stepped line is where the front wing overlaps the rear, forming what looks like a single left-side wing, as on a real moth. I'd guess that this is just part of what was originally a carving of a whole moth. See, this little bit of edge here is unpolished and rough, where these left wings have broken off from the body.'

'I think you're right,' said Wilfred. 'Now that you've pointed it out, I can see that it does look just like the wings of one of those big tropical moths, 'specially if you imagine the opposite wings and a body between. I always knew it reminded me of something, but I could never put my finger on it. I'll take your word for it on the particular species.'

24

'And are Malaysian moon moths black?' asked Marcia.

'Well, no; they're bright yellow with brown markings,' said Professor Gadling. 'But this carving's blackness is easily explained by the simple fact that the artist was working with jet. It's a colourless sculpture.'

'So all these weird lined markings represent the brown pattern you'd find on these moths?' said Ben.

'Hmm . . . well, actually,' said Professor Gadling, 'this pattern really doesn't match any markings that *I've* ever seen on a moon moth. It's the only thing that doesn't look biologically accurate. But, having said that, markings vary considerably between different regional subspecies across Southeast Asia, so it could be that this depicts a subspecies unique to Pulau Gigi Naga of which I'm unaware. Or the lined pattern could simply be artistic licence.'

'Whatever the case,' said Professor Hartleigh-Broadbeam, 'the species of early human that sculpted this clearly had very sophisticated artistic and tool-handling abilities.'

'That's what I realised when I found it,' said Wilfred, returning to his story. 'I didn't know anything then about the different types of early man or how long ago they lived, but I *was* sure that the skeleton and carving must be important, scientifically. So I ran back to the camp to report what I'd found to the captain who was leading the expedition. But he was a short-tempered man, with no interest in stuff like that. He'd already given the platoon orders to strike camp and move on, and he wasn't the sort of man to change his mind. All I had time to do before we left was to nip back to the cave, take the skeleton's skull and the carving, and stuff them into the bottom of my rucksack. A few days later, we'd finished our survey and were sailing back to mainland Malaya. Shortly after that, I'd completed my National Service and was back in Britain, back at my parents' home in Essex.

'I'd managed to keep the skull and carving safely in my possession and, a few days after returning home, I took a train into London to show my find to the people I'd read were Britain's top experts on early human remains: the Palaeoanthropology Department of the Royal Westminster Institute of Natural History — the very building we were at this evening. I ran up those front steps imagining how the people there would look at my find with amazement, imagining how they'd congratulate me for bringing the skull and carving back from Pulau Gigi Naga, imagining how they might even ask me to join their research team, in spite of my lack of education. But they did none of those things.'

'What did they do?' asked Marcia.

'They laughed at me,' said Wilfred quietly. 'They sneered at me and mocked my way of speaking and asked what an uneducated boy soldier would know about human evolution. They wouldn't even look at what I'd brought them; wouldn't even let me past the front desk. Told me I'd probably picked up the skull of a common orang-utan and sent me packing.' Before, as he'd been telling his story of finding the skeleton, Wilfred had seemed to grow more confident in manner. But now he seemed to shrink back into himself once more, hunching his small shoulders and looking down at the table.

'Couldn't you have taken the skull and the moth-wing carving to experts somewhere else?' asked Sam.

'Yeah, there must've been other science institutes or museums that would've looked at them properly,' said Zara.

'I'd been totally humiliated,' said Wilfred. 'I couldn't face being laughed at like that a second time. I went straight back to my parents' house, put the skull and the carving away in this biscuit tin, and shoved the tin up in the attic. And that's where they stayed until just two months ago. You're the first people I've shown them to.'

'You kept this skull and this jet carving hidden in the attic for more than *fifty years*?' exclaimed Marcia.

'Surely at some point over fifty years you could have tried again,' said Ben. 'You could have shown them to *some-one* who'd have—'

'Maybe I could have, but I *didn't*, OK?' interrupted Wilfred, with sudden ferocity. '*You* would have done, but *I* didn't! You don't know what it's like to be me, and you're lucky not to know. I was a shy, scrawny little nobody who'd been bullied by my father, bullied at school and bullied in the army. I had no friends and no confidence.' The words were pouring out of him now, and the corners of his mouth were quivering as he spoke. 'Finding that skeleton was the first interesting thing that had ever happened to me, and taking the skull and the carving to the Royal West-minster Institute was the first time I'd dared to dream that I might be able to do something exciting with my life. But all I got was another slap in the face. So I shoved my dreams away in the attic and crawled back under my stone. I haven't had a successful life. Dead-end jobs. Lonely flats. Years wasted taking refuge in the bottle. You don't need to remind me how many decades have passed.'

'I'm sorry,' said Ben quickly. 'I didn't mean to.' The chil-dren all felt awful now for having pressed Wilfred for explanations.

Wilfred took a sip of water. He looked rather embarrassed now that his outburst was over. 'No, *I'm* sorry for being so self-pitying and rude,' he said to Ben. 'Unforgivable. You must all be wishing you'd never asked me to join you here.'

'No, we don't think that!' said Ben, really worried that Wilfred might be about to leave.

'No indeed,' said Professor Gadling, patting Wilfred on the shoulder. 'And we're honoured that you decided to show the skull and the carving to *us*. Ah – here comes the food!'

Zara wondered what the waiters would make of seeing a skull on the table, but Wilfred hurriedly put it away as they approached.

Soon everyone had a plate of pizza or bowl of pasta in front of them. Once the waiters had departed and everyone was digging in hungrily, Wilfred continued his story. 'Two months ago', he said, 'my mother died. My father died decades back, but she'd lived on into her nineties. A few days after her funeral, as I was clearing out all the stuff from her council house, I came across the biscuit tin, still up in the attic where I'd put it. And as I sat there, holding the skull and the carving in my hands again, something made me decide that I was finally going to get to the bottom of what they were. But this time I wasn't going to take them to any more experts. Somehow, at that moment in the attic, with my mother just gone, it seemed important that for once in my life I should take charge of something myself. I decided to make *myself* an expert. Or at least to make myself knowledgeable.

'So, over the last two months, I've educated myself. I've read all the library books I can find on human evolution and I've visited dozens of museum collections of early human fossils. I've bought myself a computer and taught myself how to look stuff up on the internet. I've learnt how scientists categorise all the different species of early human, and how they identify the remains they dig up.'

Wilfred reached into his bag and pulled out a large library book entitled *Human Evolution*. He flipped through, then opened it flat on the table at a page that had drawings of early human species arranged on an evolutionary diagram.

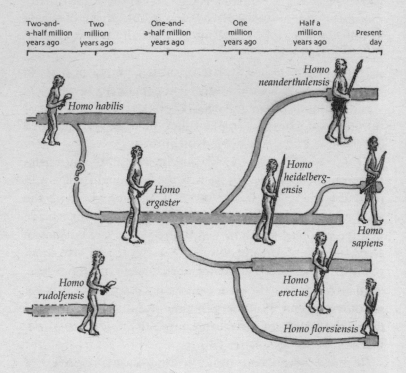

'This page gives a good overview of all the different human species that archaeologists have discovered,' said Wilfred, his manner of speaking becoming ever more confident as he began sharing his newly acquired knowledge of the subject. 'As you can see,' he pointed out to the children, 'these species are all called *Homo* something. *Homo* is Latin for human, and is what scientists call the genus name – the sort of group name – for all human species. The second word of these scientific names denotes the particular species. Scientists call our own species *Homo sapiens*. *Sapiens* is Latin for wise. Of course, all humans on the planet today are *Homo sapiens* – all members of the one single species. We're the only species of the *Homo* genus that still exists.'

'I've never been sure that "wise human" was an appropriate choice of name,' growled Professor Gauntraker, 'considering some of the things our species has got up to.'

Sam studied the diagram, and started to make sense of it. 'So some of these early human species – like *Homo heidelbergensis* – were our direct ancestors?' he said.

'The experts think so, yes,' said Wilfred. 'Whereas other species are believed to be more like evolutionary cousins of ours – species that branched off from one of our direct ancestor species and evolved differently.'

'Like the Neanderthals?' said Zara, spotting *Homo neanderthalensis* on the diagram.

'Yes,' said Wilfred. 'Most scientists agree that the Neanderthals were our closest evolutionary cousins. They were an older species than us, but they were still around for many thousands of years after our own species evolved, sharing part of the planet with us.'

'It must have been weird having another species of human around as well as us,' said Ben.

'It probably wouldn't have seemed weird to our *Homo sapiens* ancestors,' said Professor Gadling. 'The idea seems weird to us now because we've got so used to being the only human species left. But our species' situation is relatively unusual in nature. Most species of animal share their particular genus group with other living species. There are two quite different species of chimpanzee, for instance, six species of flamingo, and at least forty-four species of sea horse, to give just a few examples off the top of my head.'

'But *why* are we the only human species left?' asked Zara. 'What happened to species like the Neanderthals? When did they all die out? And why?'

'It's reckoned that the very last Neanderthals probably died out about twenty-five thousand years ago,' said Wilfred. 'As for *why* the species died out, scientists don't really know. They may have been unable to compete for food once *Homo sapiens* moved into Europe, the Neanderthals' region; they may have been less good at adapting to climate changes at the end of the last Ice Age; they may have been hit by diseases that *Homo sapiens* were more resistant to. And some scientists think that *Homo sapiens* may have wiped out the Neanderthals by deliberately killing them.'

'Yeah, that sounds like the way our species usually behaves,' muttered Marcia.

Sam hoped that this last theory wasn't the correct one. It was a horrible thing to think of your own ancestors doing, even if it had happened twenty-five thousand years ago.

'What about this species, *Homo floresiensis*?' said Marcia, pointing to the diagram. 'From this, it looks like *they* were still around more recently than the Neanderthals.'

'Is that the species of those really small skeletons that

were discovered just a few years ago on the island of Flores, in Indonesia?' asked Ben, remembering something he'd seen on television. 'The one they said was the size of a hobbit.'

'That's the one,' said Wilfred. 'Scientists are still arguing about it, but if the archaeologists who found it are right, it was probably a relative of *Homo erectus*. It may have gone extinct for similar reasons to the Neanderthals, though scientists have found a more obvious likely cause – evidence of a huge volcanic eruption on Flores about twelve thousand years ago. *Homo floresiensis* was much smaller-brained than us or the Neanderthals, but even so, the discovery that another human species might have still been around as recently as that caused a right stir.'

'Yes indeed,' said Professor Hartleigh-Broadbeam. She turned to the children. 'Twelve thousand years ago may not *sound* very recent, but in terms of the millions of years of human evolution, it's the blinking of an eye.'

'Anyway, Wilfred,' said Professor Gadling, 'the big question is: have you managed to identify the skeleton you found? To which of these early human species did it belong?'

Wilfred paused before answering. 'I know I'm only a beginner to this subject,' he said, 'but I've been thorough in my research. And I've discovered three things about the early human whose skeleton I found in that cave. Things that seem almost unbelievable. Things that will cause a much, much bigger stir than the discovery of *Homo floresiensis*.'

Wilfred opened his biscuit tin and brought the skull back out. 'The first thing I've discovered,' he said, 'is that this skull doesn't match the skulls of any previously known early human species.' He flipped over the page of the book, revealing a series of photographs of skulls – one for each of the early human species known to science.

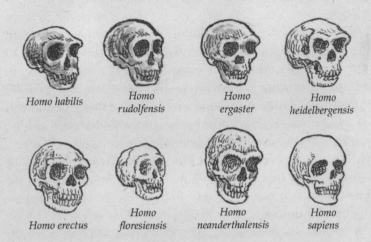

Homo habilis

Homo rudolfensis

Homo ergaster

Homo heidelbergensis

Homo erectus

Homo floresiensis

Homo neanderthalensis

Homo sapiens

Wilfred ran his hand over the top of the skull. 'This skull's cranium is as large and domed as a *Homo sapiens* cranium,' he pointed out, 'which suggests it had a *Homo sapiens*-sized brain. That alone rules out nearly all of the known early human species. Only the Neanderthals had craniums and brains as big as ours. But this definitely isn't a Neanderthal skull.' He pointed to the Neanderthal skull photo. 'You can see that Neanderthal skulls have prominent brow ridges, big nose holes and large front teeth. This skull that I found has none of those.'

'You're right!' agreed Professor Gadling. 'This skull you found, with its twin cranial ridges, its unusually large eye sockets and its small lower face, bears no resemblance to any of the skulls in this book.'

'I've checked every book and museum I can,' said Wilfred, 'and I'm certain that this skull looks nothing like any 'other skull that's ever been found.'

'Good lord!' said Professor Hartleigh-Broadbeam.

'The second thing I've discovered', Wilfred went on, 'is that no known species of early human is thought to have been capable of making something this complex.' He held up the jet carving of the moth wings. 'A lot of early human species made tools and weapons, and the Neanderthals may have made some very basic stone sculptures, but archaeologists have only *ever* found carvings as sophisticated as this at *Homo sapiens* sites. We're supposed to be the only species who's ever produced art of anything like this quality.'

'So we're talking about a previously unknown species of early human that seems to have been as large-brained and culturally sophisticated as our own species!' exclaimed Professor Gauntraker. 'Astonishing!'

'It gets more astonishing,' said Wilfred. 'The third thing I've discovered about the skeleton I found is how long ago the individual it belonged to died.'

'You mean you've had a radiocarbon-dating test run on the skull?' asked Professor Ampersand.

'Yeah,' confirmed Wilfred. 'As you probably know, many museums and universities have specialist radiocarbon-dating labs and, two weeks ago, I managed to find the address of one such lab which offers a testing service to the public, for a fee. I didn't want to show anyone the whole skull, but at the bottom of the biscuit tin, I'd found a small fragment of bone that must have flaked off from the skull at some point. I posted the fragment to the lab, along with the necessary payment, and I got the result back just a few days ago. According to the test, this skull is only about five thousand years old.'

For a second or two there was a stunned silence.

'Only five thousand years old?' echoed Professor

35

Hartleigh-Broadbeam. 'But that's *impossibly* recent! Five thousand years ago is within the era of recorded history – within the era of proper human civilisations: cities . . . pyramids . . . the development of writing . . . the invention of the wheel. Are you really saying that as recently as that, an entirely different but equally intelligent species of human was still sharing the planet with us, living on this remote island of Gigi Naga?'

'I know it sounds almost unbelievable,' said Wilfred, 'but I can't think of any other explanation to fit everything I've discovered.'

'Well, you told us you were going to show us something really extraordinary, Wilfred, but that was an understatement!' declared Professor Gadling. 'This will rewrite the science books, the history books and the encyclopaedias! This could be the scientific discovery of the decade! One of the scientific discoveries of the century!'

'I know,' said Wilfred. 'But I need to prove it.'

'Aren't the skull and the carving all the proof you need?' asked Zara.

'Not quite,' said Wilfred. 'Experts could say that this skull was merely that of a *Homo sapiens* who was affected by some unusual deformity of the head. Or that it was an ordinary *Homo sapiens* skull that I'd altered myself. And they could argue that this carving was a piece of *Homo sapiens* art that I'd found elsewhere. They could say that we only have my word for it that I found this carving in the cave with the skeleton, that we only have my word for it that the skeleton and the cave existed at all. And they'd be right to be suspicious; there have been plenty of hoaxes and mistakes in this field of research before. No, I need further proof and—and, well, I'm hoping you professors might be able to help me.' He turned to Professor Gadling, seeming nervous once more. 'When I saw the advertisement for your lecture, I remembered reading about you and your colleagues, and an idea came into my head. It's probably a stupid, ridiculous idea, but I decided to come and see you tonight anyway, to try and show you my skull and carving and to put my idea to you.'

'What, exactly,' said Professor Gadling, 'are you proposing?'

'An expedition,' said Wilfred. 'I want to organise my own small-scale, independent expedition to Pulau Gigi Naga, and . . . er . . . I thought you'd be the perfect team to help me: an open-minded naturalist and a renowned explorer, both with experience of working in tropical rainforests; and the operators of a small flying boat that would be ideal for getting us to the small lake, close to the cave.'

From the bottom of the biscuit tin, Wilfred brought out a rolled-up sheet of old, yellowing paper, and unfurled it on the desk, revealing a hand-drawn map of an island.

'This is Pulau Gigi Naga,' said Wilfred. 'I drew this copy back in 1954 from the map our platoon made. As I said, we only made a brief survey, so only a few major features are marked, but I haven't been able to find any more detailed maps of the island. It was never actually used for anything by the British, even after our platoon surveyed it. And the Malaysians, who've owned it since the 1960s, have left it as a nature reserve. Apart from the occasional visiting naturalist, no one's been there for years, and I've read that most of the rainforest covering the island remains completely unexplored. But, as you can see, the position of the lake is marked. Once we'd landed there, I'm sure I could find the cave again. We'd need to find the skeleton and excavate the rest of the cave properly – find other skeletons if they're there, and find other carvings and artefacts and tools. We'd

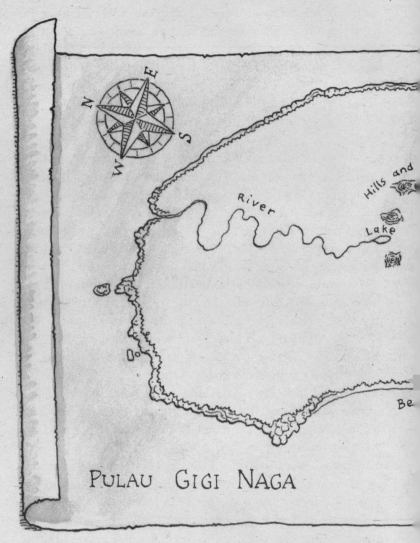

PULAU GIGI NAGA

need to establish beyond any doubt that there really was a whole population of a genuinely different species of human living on Pulau Gigi Naga. Then, and only then, would we

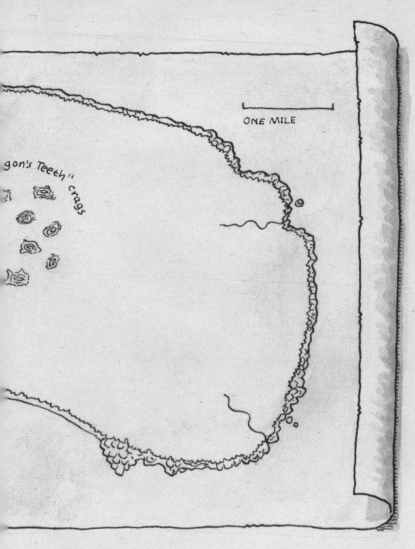

ONE MILE

gon's Teeth" crags

present our findings to the world.' He paused again and looked hesitantly around the table at everyone. 'I—I know I don't have experience of organising expeditions, but I really want to do this. My mother left me a few thousand pounds. I know that's not really enough to run an expedition to the other side of the world, but maybe it would be enough to get us started. It's all I have to offer you. What do you think?'

5

Just looking at the map made Ben's insides tingle. A tropical island on the other side of the world. Unexplored rainforest. A cave that possibly contained more extraordinary human remains. The chance to be in on one of the scientific discoveries of the century. Surely the adults *had* to agree to Wilfred's proposal. He exchanged a glance with Zara, Sam and Marcia, seeing in their eyes the same eager excitement that he felt. And he sensed that the same crucial question was going through each of their four heads: if the adults *did* agree to make an expedition to Pulau Gigi Naga, was there any chance that they would be allowed to go too?

'An expedition!' said Professor Hartleigh-Broadbeam. She turned to Professor Gauntraker. 'You're the exploration expert, Eric. Do you think such an expedition is feasible?'

Professor Gauntraker paused for a moment before replying. 'The jungles of Southeast Asia', he growled, speaking slowly and dramatically, 'are some of the most inhospitable and unexplored environments on earth. On an island such as Gigi Naga, one can expect to encounter temperatures that'll drive the strongest man out of his mind, humidity levels that'll rot the shirt from your back and the skin from your feet, army ants as big as your thumb, leeches that'll suck your blood 'til they're the size of aubergines, and species of venomous snake and spider for whose bite there is no known antidote. An expedition to such a remote and difficult destination on the sort of shoestring budget that Wilfred's proposing would defeat most of the world's hardiest explorers.'

Wilfred sighed and let go the edges of his map, allowing it to roll up once more. 'I understand,' he said sadly. 'You're the expert, and if you think we really shouldn't go—'

'*Shouldn't go?*' exclaimed Professor Gauntraker. 'Of course we should go! I wouldn't miss out on a challenge like this for the world!' He sounded astonished that Wilfred could have misconstrued his list of glorious hardships and dangers as things that anyone would want to avoid.

'Well *I'm* certainly up for making this expedition,' declared Professor Gadling. 'It's vital that this cave is properly investigated.'

'I'm as excited by the idea as you two are,' said Professor Ampersand. 'But don't forget that Petunia and I can't drop everything and dash off round the world quite as easily as you. We've got Zara, Ben and Marcia to consider.'

'Bring 'em with us!' said Professor Gauntraker. 'And Sam too, of course.' He turned to Wilfred. 'The newspaper reports you read of this summer's events played down the crucial role these children played. There were ongoing concerns for their security and privacy, you understand. But believe me, they're the most resourceful, courageous and sensible young people you could ever hope to meet. They'd be a great asset to any expedition.'

'Yes, I'm sure they would,' agreed Wilfred enthusiastically. 'Honestly, I–I'd be happy with whatever plan you all think best.' He seemed quite dazed to find that his proposition for an expedition was actually being taken up.

Ben's head was tingling: partly a blushing tingle caused by Professor Gauntraker's complimentary words, but mostly a tingle of excitement triggered by the suggestion the explorer had made. He glanced at Zara, Sam and Marcia again, and they all looked at Professor Ampersand and Professor Hartleigh-Broadbeam.

'I'm all in favour of taking everybody on this expedition,' said Professor Ampersand. 'The only thing is, we can't *all* get to Pulau Gigi Naga in the *Silver Turtle*. She only seats five people, remember – six at an absolute limit.'

'Hmm, you're right,' said Professor Gauntraker. 'We'd have to charter a small ship as well. It'd take us much longer to get there, of course.'

'Or couldn't we find a second aircraft?' suggested Sam.

'Yeah,' said Marcia. 'What about Gabrielle and Hank's airship?' She was referring to Gabrielle Starling and Hank Zootlin, a pair of veteran aviators, both in their eighties, whom they had met during their last adventure. They lived aboard an airship, travelling the world. Gabrielle was a remarkable woman, who had worked as a pilot all over the world.

'Hank's airship might be a little slow for our purposes,' said Professor Gadling, 'and anyway, I believe Hank and his craft are fully occupied helping out with an environmental project in Brazil. I suppose what we *really* need is a bigger flying boat, but there aren't many of them still in operation.'

'But maybe Gabrielle would know someone who's got one,' said Ben.

'You're right!' declared Professor Gauntraker. 'If anyone

can find us a large flying boat we can hire cheaply, Gabrielle can. She might even be able to come and pilot it herself. Excellent thinking, you three! Now this whole plan's beginning to take shape!'

Fired with an energetic enthusiasm, his deep-set eyes gleaming in the candlelight, Professor Gauntraker spread out Wilfred's map of the island once more and pinned down its four corners with cutlery and glasses. 'Look,' he said, picking up a small salt pot and a large pepper grinder and swooping them over the table together, 'we fly the *Silver Turtle* and the larger flying boat out to Southeast Asia in convoy. From the map, the lake looks much too small to land a large flying boat on, so when we get to Gigi Naga, we land both planes here.' He plonked the salt pot and pepper grinder down on the map, in a wide bay on the western side of the island's coastline. 'We'd anchor the large flying boat in the bay and use her as an offshore base, to sleep on each night. We'd use the *Silver Turtle* to ferry us and our equipment up to the lake each morning', he continued, enacting this short flight with the salt pot, 'and then back to the large flying boat each evening. It'll take two or three trips to ferry us all each time, but that's OK; it's only a few miles. This scheme will save days of hacking our way through difficult terrain, and also save us having to camp out at nights in the jungle itself – an uncomfortable business for those of you not used to it.'

'It's a good plan,' said Professor Ampersand. 'It would take us a few days to fly out to Southeast Asia in the first place – the *Silver Turtle*'s top speed is only 250 miles per hour – but that needn't be a problem; no doubt we can arrange places to make overnight stops along the route. If we're planning to sleep on board the big flying boat each night, all we'd really need would be places where we could land safely and get the planes refuelled and recharged.'

'Garrulous and I have got plenty of old friends all over the world who can help to arrange that,' said Professor Gauntraker. 'And we should get Ivy onto that side of things too, with all her high-level international contacts.' He was referring to Professor Ivy Sharpe, an old friend who worked as an environmental biologist for the United Nations in Geneva. 'She should also be able to help us get authorisation from the Malaysian authorities to go into Pulau Gigi Naga; the days when Western expeditions felt they could just barge into other countries' territory without permission are long gone, and a good thing too. Ivy might be too busy to come on the expedition itself, though.'

'Even if she is, Adam must come with us,' said Marcia. Adam was a young orphan they'd encountered on their first adventure, who had recently been adopted by Professor Sharpe.

'Of course,' agreed Professor Gadling, 'and if we're rounding up old friends for this expedition, we ought to see if Bob Pottle wants to get involved. Professor Pottle's another of our old colleagues you probably read about,' he said to Wilfred. 'An excellent fellow. I must say you were right to come to us with this proposition, Wilfred. With our experience and contacts, and your expertise in early human remains, we're the perfect expedition team.'

'The only thing I think we may be missing', said Professor Gauntraker, 'is someone with experience of archaeological excavation – someone who knows how to dig up fossils and artefacts correctly without damaging them, and how to catalogue them. If we're to impress the scientific establishment with our findings, the excavation of the cave needs to be done expertly. You've clearly acquired plenty of knowledge on the subject of early human remains, Wilfred, but would I be right in thinking you don't have much actual experience of digging such remains up?'

'You're right,' said Wilfred, looking suddenly deflated again. 'I wouldn't know how to organise the dig properly. I was hoping one of you might have experience of such things. Maybe the whole idea's not practical after all.'

'Nonsense!' exclaimed Professor Gauntraker. 'It's not a big problem. I just meant we'll have to recruit someone for that job. I'm sure we can find ourselves an archaeologist.'

Wilfred looked immensely relieved. He'd really expected the whole plan to collapse over such a minor problem, realised Zara. He must have had so many knock-backs in his life that he couldn't actually believe anything he started would succeed. She was glad they were helping this man finally to achieve his dream.

'Of course, the archaeologist would have to be someone we can trust to be discreet until we're ready to show the world your discovery,' added Professor Gauntraker. 'And that need for discretion goes for all of us. We must keep Wilfred's find a secret and keep all our general plans for the expedition fairly quiet, too. If word of this gets out before we can get to Gigi Naga, others might beat us to it – either clumsy amateurs who could wreck the site, or unscrupulous experts who'd claim the discovery for themselves. Now,' he continued, 'we'll need to organise ourselves quickly. I'd like to be ready to leave in three weeks' time, in the second week of October. I think we should plan for the expedition to last about three weeks in total, to allow us time to get there, find the cave, make some sort of excavation, and return home. If we leave it much past the end of October, we'll be into the winter monsoon season, and stand a higher chance of being hit by storms.'

'Leave in three weeks' time?' said Professor Hartleigh-Broadbeam. 'But the young people are at school during October, apart from their one week's half-term break.'

'Then let 'em extend their break by a couple of weeks,' said Professor Gauntraker, firmly. 'They'll learn more on this trip than they would in any classroom.'

'That's probably true,' agreed Professor Ampersand.

The children grinned at one another, almost unable to believe how well this discussion was going.

'Well, I suppose all their schools *might* give them permission,' conceded Professor Hartleigh-Broadbeam, 'as long as they take some schoolwork with them. However, I'm afraid *I* wouldn't be able to come with you during those dates. I've got several very important conferences and meetings to attend. But I'll certainly give all the help and support I can on the organisation side.'

'That's fine, Petunia,' said Professor Gauntraker. 'It's always good to have someone competent back home, co-ordinating things. We'll make your flat the expedition office. Now, I think we've covered everything. I'll sum up the expedition team as I see it. Somebody get this down. Have you got a notebook and pencil on you, Sam?'

Sam, as usual, did. He leafed through to find a page that wasn't covered with one of his invention ideas, and as Professor Gauntraker rattled off the personnel list, he wrote it down:

Expedition founder, guide and palaeoanthropologist: Wilfred Lugg.
Expedition Leader: Professor Eric Gauntraker.
Chief naturalist: Professor Garrulous Gadling.
Chief engineer: Professor Alexander Ampersand.

Assistant engineer (if he can come): Professor Bob Pottle.

Pilots: Amy McAirdrie and Gabrielle Starling (if she'll come).

Expedition crew: Sam, Zara, Ben, Marcia and Adam.

Expedition archeologist: To be appointed.

Expedition UK manager: Professor Petunia Hartleigh-Broadbeam.

International co-ordinator: Professor Ivy Sharpe.

'Sounds like a pretty good team to me,' said Professor Gadling. He raised his wine glass. 'To the Pulau Gigi Naga Expedition.'

'And to the scientific discovery of the decade,' added Professor Hartleigh-Broadbeam.

'And to Wilfred,' proposed Professor Ampersand.

As everyone echoed Professor Ampersand's toast, Wilfred looked as if he might burst, his lined face breaking into a clearly unfamiliar expression of happiness. 'Thank you, everyone,' he managed to blurt out hoarsely.

The four children all felt they might burst too – burst with excitement. In just three weeks, they would be setting off on an expedition to a virtually unexplored tropical island on the other side of the world.

A great many things were organised during the next three weeks.

The first priority for Sam, of course, was to get his parents' agreement for him to go on the trip, and this they gave. His mum said that after all the chaotic travels that Sam and his friends had been thrown into previously, it would be a pleasant change to know they were going on an entirely planned expedition.

Professor Sharpe was contacted, and, although she was too busy to come on the expedition herself, she readily agreed that Adam should go.

Professor Pottle also turned out to be unavailable to go, as he was helping to organise an important conference on his specialist subject – animal-dung-based fuel systems. However, he sent them a urine-powered combined-fan-and-insect-repeller that he'd invented, which he said would be invaluable in areas without mains electricity.

The five children's four schools all granted permission for the children to add an extra two weeks to their half-term breaks, on the condition that they took some school-work with them.

The most important thing that needed to be organised was the transport, and Gabrielle, their veteran pilot friend, was contacted the morning after the decisive meeting in the restaurant. (Her airship home was fully equipped with email.) She replied immediately, agreeing with great enthusiasm to join their expedition and stating that she knew of a large amphibious flying boat that would be perfect for their purposes, which she was sure they'd be able to borrow.

Professor Sharpe obtained permission from the Malaysian authorities for them to conduct a scientific expedition to Pulau Gigi Naga, without needing to be specific about what they hoped to find. She also arranged many of the overnight-stop locations for the two flying boats on their long journey there and back. Other stopover places were arranged by Professor Gauntraker, Professor Gadling and Gabrielle.

Professor Gadling began their search for an expedition archaeologist by contacting a university archaeology lecturer he knew. She highly recommended one of her recent students, a young man named Simon Arblinton who, as luck would have it, was already working in Southeast Asia, helping to excavate a temple in Thailand. He was, she said, bright, hard-working, likeable and trustworthy. A series of emails between Professor Gadling and Simon established that Simon would be willing to take some time off from the temple excavation in order to join their expedition. Simon's emails expressed great excitement about Wilfred's discovery, though he assured Professor Gadling that, as instructed, he wouldn't discuss the matter with anyone else at this stage. They arranged that Simon would meet them in Peninsular Malaysia, at the flying boats' last overnight stopover destination before Pulau Gigi Naga itself.

Sam came to stay at the flat for both weekends prior to the departure date. Professor Gauntraker took him and Marcia all over London to obtain the equipment and supplies they required. Aware that they'd need to keep back a lot of their meagre budget for travelling costs such as fuel, they were careful with the money, buying things cheaply from second-hand sources or borrowing items from explorer friends.

Everything they acquired was stored at Professor Hartleigh-Broadbeam's tiny London flat – the expedition headquarters. Sam and Marcia felt more and more excited as the entire place became taken over by preparations for the expedition. Every inch of the living room floor was soon covered with growing piles of equipment and provisions: camping stoves, lightweight pans, cooking utensils, crates of tinned food, water containers, toolboxes, dusty pickaxes and shovels, three steel-bladed machetes (for hacking through rainforest vegetation), heavy-duty torches and hurricane lamps, coils of climbing rope, a small inflatable rubber boat, wooden paddles, and much else besides. The computer desk became buried beneath an avalanche of lists, schedules and maps. The floors of both bedrooms disappeared under heaps of clothing, toiletries and medical supplies. Even the bathroom was pressed into service, with the shower rail being used to air some musty old mosquito nets that Professor Gauntraker had bought for next to nothing from a retired missionary.

The kitchen table became a workbench, at which Sam used his practical skills to make any necessary repairs to second-hand pieces of equipment. Some of the oldest items looked beyond fixing, but these were the challenges Sam enjoyed most, and he nearly always found a way to make them serviceable again.

Wilfred came to the flat every day, eagerly helping with whatever he could. From time to time, he would take the skull out of his old biscuit tin for everyone to muse on further.

They also continued to examine the piece of jet carving. The more Sam looked at the complex pattern on the moon moth wing, the more he felt that the grooved lines had been etched with real deliberation and precision, rather than simply artistic flair. It was hard to put his finger on why, but each line in the pattern looked as if it *mattered*, somehow – as if it *had* to be where it was. But although this suggested that the mysterious prehistoric sculptor had been concerned primarily with accuracy, Professor Gadling remained certain that the lines resembled no moth-wing pattern he'd ever seen.

Zara and Ben were back in Edinburgh for all this time, attending school during the week but helping Professor Ampersand and Amy make some improvements to the *Silver Turtle* during evenings and weekends, out at Amy's hangar. These improvements included a pilot's radio and extra energy cells to increase the plane's range. Professor Ampersand was also working on an electric outboard motor to power the expedition's inflatable boat.

On the huge world map on his bedroom wall, Ben marked their planned route to Pulau Gigi Naga with a thick pencil line, and marked all their ports of call along it with tantalising little name stickers.

Shortly after sending her first email, Gabrielle sent another, confirming that the loan of the plane was all fixed up, and saying that she'd also arranged the use of the runway and facilities at a flying club she knew near London, in Kent. It was decided that they would rendezvous at this flying club the day before setting off, with Gabrielle bringing the big plane, and Amy bringing herself and the three Ampersands down from Scotland in the *Silver Turtle*. The others (including Adam) would bring all the supplies and equipment from the London flat. They would get the big plane loaded up by the evening, sleep on board, and be ready to take off at the crack of dawn.

At last, the day before their departure date arrived. Professor Gauntraker had borrowed an old delivery van, which he parked outside the flat. They had just finished loading everything into it when a taxi pulled up, from which Professor Ivy Sharpe and Adam emerged.

Professor Sharpe was a petite, smartly dressed woman in her early sixties. She cast a critical eye into the back of the van. 'Well, you seem to have organised the equipment reasonably competently, at least,' she said, sounding surprised that they hadn't made a complete hash of it without her help. 'Now, has everybody remembered to pack their passports and visas? And you have all had your immunisation jabs, haven't you? And, Eric, I hope you haven't lost that list of contact telephone numbers I sent you.'

'Sorry about Mum,' whispered Adam to his friends. 'She'd be more relaxed if she was coming too. It's only because she worries about us.'

'We know,' said Sam, grinning. 'It's OK.' They were all used to Professor Sharpe's ultra-efficiency by now.

'We wouldn't even be able to *get* to Pulau Gigi Naga if

it wasn't for the things she's organised,' said Marcia.

Adam smiled with pride for his adoptive mother. When Sam and Marcia had first met Adam six months ago, he'd been a sad, ghostly pale boy, afflicted by the most disturbing start in life imaginable. It was great to see how happy and confident he was these days in his new life with Professor Sharpe. He was still an unusual child, with an extraordinary genetic make-up. Although he looked about nine or ten, he was actually very much younger. And he possessed some advanced mental and physical abilities. But he displayed these abilities rarely and modestly, and his most prominent traits were the ones he'd developed for himself: kindness, loyalty and courage.

Once the six expedition members had given Professors Hartleigh-Broadbeam and Sharpe a goodbye hug and kiss, they squeezed into the van with all the equipment and set off.

As the van moved off, an ordinary-looking dark-blue car pulled away from the kerb a few hundred metres back along the street, where it had been parked all day. The car's driver kept his distance, allowing other vehicles to get between himself and the van as he followed it on its journey out of London.

It was about half-past three when the van arrived at the flying club. The little aerodrome was situated in a quiet patch of countryside, and consisted of a simple tarmac runway fringed on one side by three buildings: two hangars and a long, low clubhouse with a small, square control tower on top. It was a typically damp and windy October afternoon, with the odd drop of rain spitting down from low grey clouds, and there didn't seem to be much flying going on. But there, taxiing over to a space by one of the hangars to join the other small aircraft parked there, was a small amphibious flying boat that had clearly just landed – the *Silver Turtle*.

As Professor Gauntraker pulled up beside the clubhouse, Sam watched the little plane come to a standstill with a

feeling of affection – the little plane that he and the others had helped to build, the little plane that had taken them safely through so many dangers. Amy McAirdrie's design was both beautiful and unorthodox. The aircraft's tailless body was the size and shape of a small motorboat, with its cockpit topped by a Plexiglas canopy. There was also a hatch in the stubby nose, with its own fold-up windscreen and a seat, in which Zara was now sitting. The plane's wing was an elegant swept-back crescent, held above the canopy by two streamlined struts. Built into the front of the wing were the plane's two electric motors. These motors were powered by a special kind of rechargeable energy cell, also invented by Professor Ampersand. Quite a few of the flying-club members had come out of the clubhouse to see the unusual aircraft arrive, and Sam felt proud to be associated with the plane and its inventors.

Sam, Marcia and Adam hurried over to the *Silver Turtle* as the Ampersands and Amy clambered out.

'Did you ride in the nose-hatch seat the whole way?' Marcia asked Zara.

'Yeah,' said Zara, keeping her scarf and coat hood up round her face and slapping her gloved hands together. 'A bit cold, but worth it for the open view. We can take turns to sit there on the way to Pulau Gigi Naga.'

'Was that *you* landing?' Sam asked Ben. 'Or Amy?' The *Silver Turtle* had dual controls and Ben had been sitting in the co-pilot's seat. He could fly the plane quite well, having been taught by Gabrielle during their recent adventure.

'Amy let me have the controls for some of the flight,' said Ben, grinning. 'But she did the take-off and landing.'

'I'm sure Ben could have landed just fine,' said Amy, 'but I thought it best tae be on the safe side.' Amy McAirdrie was a short, slightly stocky woman of twenty-one, with a pleasant, round face and long pale hair tied back in a straggly ponytail. 'I'll give you all some flying lessons on the way out to Southeast Asia,' she promised, 'whenever the flying conditions are safe enough.'

The flying-club secretary — an old friend of Gabrielle — came over and introduced himself. He invited them into the clubhouse and rustled up some tea and biscuits as they waited for Gabrielle to arrive. After a few minutes, the control tower reported that they had radio contact with her, and everyone went outside to watch the skies.

7

No one exactly knew what make of aeroplane Gabrielle was bringing. In her emails she'd simply said it was a rare type, but one that would meet their requirements perfectly. They could hear the aircraft above the clouds before they could see it. The noise started as a distant low hum, which then crescendoed to a growling, clattering roar.

And there it was: a huge, white, gull-winged, three-engined amphibious flying boat, emerging from the bottom of the clouds some distance away and banking round to make its approach to the runway, its big wheels already down. Sam studied the aircraft through his binoculars. Its front end was topped by a multi-curved glazed cockpit canopy that had the appearance of an elaborate botanical glasshouse. Through it, he could see the wiry figure of Gabrielle at the controls. The plane's hull was whale-shaped: bulky in the middle and becoming narrow at the rear, as it curved up to a high, double-finned tail.

The plane touched down in a perfect three-point landing, rumbled along the runway, then taxied round to park behind the *Silver Turtle*. A small side-door behind the cockpit flipped open, an aluminium ladder unfolded, and Gabrielle climbed down.

'Sorry ter be cutting it a tad fine with the time,' she rasped, as everyone greeted her with handshakes and hugs.

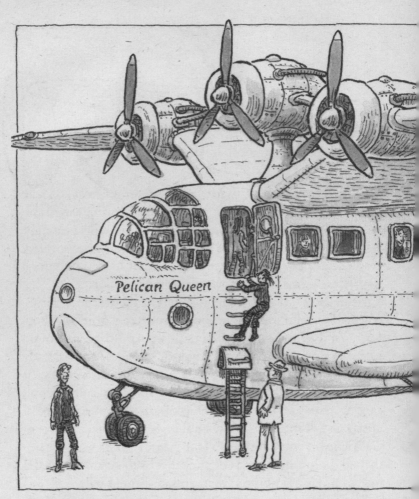

'I've just flown from Stockholm and I hit a bit of a head-wind over the North Sea.' She removed her old leather fly-ing helmet, letting her dishevelled white hair fall down around her sharp, birdlike face. 'This is the *Pelican Queen*,' she said, pointing to the aircraft's name painted in stylish blue lettering on each side of the nose. 'She's a McCay M-10.

THE PELICAN QUEEN

A Canadian make, but this one's spent most of her days in the Baltic. A Swedish pal of mine, Leif Andersen, used ter run a fleet of three of them as a charter cruise business back in the fifties and sixties. Leif's long retired, but he's kept the *Pelican Queen* on in flying condition. And he said he's so glad ter see her making another long-distance trip after all these years that we can borrow her for free, as long as we get her back ter him with the fuel tanks full.'

'Excellent!' said Professor Gadling.

'She's not the newest or most elegant plane you ever saw,' continued Gabrielle, 'but Leif says she's a reliable old crate. And she's speedy enough for us, too; she can match the *Silver Turtle*'s top speed of 250 miles per hour. So what d'you think of her?'

'Brilliant!' said Sam, and the others added their enthusiastic agreement. The *Pelican Queen* certainly looked reliable. Every part of her – the three bulky, oil-streaked engines, the heavily riveted panelling, the chunky portholes along her side – had a sturdy, workmanlike appearance.

'Come and have a look inside,' said Gabrielle.

Eagerly, the children climbed aboard and explored the plane from nose to tail: the spacious glazed cockpit, where every surface was crammed with black-and-white dials and Bakelite switches; a cubby-hole office, with a desk and map drawers; a wide communal lounge, with little tables and comfortable seats by the windows; a compact kitchen; some even more compact shower-rooms and toilets; a long central corridor with a series of neat little bedroom cabins either side, each one fitted with a pair of fold-down bunk-beds; circular floor hatchways with ladders leading down from the corridor to the lower section of the hull, where they found a spacious cargo hold, a series of shelved storerooms and a small but well-equipped repair workshop; and lastly, a tapering tunnel leading up through the plane's tail section to a tiny glazed observation bubble between the tail fins. All the different smells of the plane's interior – oily metal, electronics, old leather and fabric, polished wood, sea water – combined into an evocative scent of travel and adventure.

Soon the adults had checked the *Pelican Queen* over as well, and were as enthusiastic about her as the children. Wilfred seemed sixty years younger as he scurried around the plane, marvelling at every feature, fixture and fitting. He seemed quite overwhelmed, now that this final component of the expedition plan had actually fallen into place.

'Admittedly, the *Pelican Queen*'s not quite as ecologically friendly as yer *Silver Turtle*,' said Gabrielle, 'but I don't s'pose one three-engined plane makes that much difference ter the overall rise in global warming.'

Marcia didn't think that was a good way to look at it. She'd noticed that adults often said their individual plane or car journeys weren't going to make much difference to global warming, but everyone's individual journeys added up to make a *big* difference. But she didn't argue the point. It would have been rude to do so when Gabrielle had gone to so much trouble to find them transport. And she had to admit that, apart from her carbon-emitting petrol engines, the *Pelican Queen was* a fabulous plane.

Gabrielle opened up the big cargo door near the rear of the hull and, for the next two hours, everyone worked hard to transfer all their supplies and equipment from the van to the *Pelican Queen*. Professor Gauntraker supervised the storage of everything in its correct place for the expedition (with just a little advice from Professor Sharpe). Everything they wouldn't need until they reached Pulau Gigi Naga was stowed in the cargo hold and roped securely in place. Everything they'd need during the journey itself was packed in the right place elsewhere: food in the storerooms; cooking utensils in the galley; maps in the cubbyhole office; sleeping bags and personal rucksacks in the bedroom cabins. As they were finishing the job, it began to get dark. In the soft glow of the *Pelican Queen*'s cargo-hold lamps and cabin lights, everything inside the plane looked even more magical and exciting.

With everything loaded, they all went over to the club-house for a well-earned evening meal, while the flying-club secretary organised the refuelling and recharging of the two aircraft. Then they returned to the *Pelican Queen* to get an early night.

There were six bedroom cabins. The children took the two smallest ones, nearest the tail end – Zara and Marcia in one, Sam, Ben and Adam sharing the other, with a camp-bed augmenting the two folding bunks. The six adults shared three of the other cabins, leaving a cabin free for Simon when he joined them.

'I'm glad we're sleeping here on the plane tonight,' said Zara, drawing a pair of little canvas curtains across the cabin porthole.

'Yeah,' agreed Marcia, climbing into her sleeping bag on the top bunk. 'It feels like the expedition's already started.'

They turned off the cabin light and within a few min-utes, in spite of their excitement, both girls were soundly asleep.

Clunk. Zara was woken suddenly by a noise. She fumbled in the darkness for her watch and pressed the illumination button. 2.46 a.m. *Clunk.* There it was again. A dull metallic noise, not very loud. Sounded like it was coming from the front of the plane. Maybe one of the adults was checking or fixing something. But that seemed unlikely at this hour. And anyway, the noise sounded more like a loose door or hatch cover, blowing in the wind. Should she go and check? She needed the toilet anyway, now she'd been woken.

Moving silently, to avoid disturbing Marcia's sleep, she got out of her sleeping bag, felt for her torch in a side pocket of her rucksack, and tiptoed to the cabin door. The plane's central corridor was unlit, and she could see no lights on at the front of the plane. Didn't look like any of the adults were up.

Clunk. It was definitely coming from near the cockpit. Zara switched on her torch and padded along the shadowy corridor, past the other bedroom-cabin doors. As she made her way past the galley kitchen and through the lounge, she suddenly felt a bit scared. What if it wasn't just something blowing in the wind? Should she have woken Marcia to come with her? Or one of the adults? She told herself not to be silly. Surely it wasn't very likely that anyone would be burgling a plane full of second-hand expedition equipment parked on a quiet airfield.

She entered the short passageway that led from the lounge to the cockpit. To her right was the entrance to the cubby-hole office. To her left was the plane's small side entrance door, and this, she saw, was the source of the clunking noise. The door wasn't closed properly and, as she'd guessed, the wind was making it clunk on its latch fitting. Whoever had been last to come aboard earlier must have failed to fasten it. Zara pulled it fully shut and turned the handle to click the latch into place. Then she tiptoed back through the lounge to the corridor, feeling glad she hadn't woken everybody up for nothing.

In the cubby-hole office, a black-clad, masked figure crouched in the inky shadows beneath the desk. He waited until Zara had used the toilet and gone back to her bedroom cabin, waited ten minutes more, then slipped silently from his hiding place and left the office. He tiptoed to the aircraft's side-door — the door through which he had entered the plane shortly before Zara had been woken by its clunking. Stealthily, he turned the handle and opened the door. He didn't unfold the aluminium ladder. Instead, with considerable agility, he clambered out onto the side of the cockpit canopy framework, next to the doorway. With a long stretch of his arm, he managed to reach across and close the door noiselessly behind him – this time making sure it was properly shut – before springing down to the tarmac below. His black, rubber-soled trainers made no sound as he sprinted away to the far edge of the airfield and disappeared into the darkness.

The next time Zara woke, it was to the sound and smell of bacon and eggs being fried. She looked at her watch. 6.35 a.m. Pulling back a porthole curtain, she saw that the sky was still dark, but blue-grey now rather than black.

Marcia's pyjama-clad legs swung down from the top bunk. 'Morning,' she said, jumping down.

The girls dressed quickly and hurried along to the kitchen, where they found Professor Ampersand frying rolls for everyone with his Portable Travel-Size Auto-Breakfast-Maker, a new invention he'd brought along to try out. 'It's a little more successful than my last breakfast machine,' he observed, 'though the flipping mechanism is maybe a wee bit on the vigorous side. Whoops, there goes another egg.'

Soon everyone was up. Zara mentioned finding the door open to Gabrielle, who thanked her for closing it and said they'd have to be more careful about shutting it properly in future.

At 7.15, just before dawn, they were ready for take-off. Marcia took first turn in the *Silver Turtle*'s co-pilot's seat next to Amy, and Sam sat in the nose-hatch seat. Professor

Gadling sat in the back, and everyone else took seats on board the *Pelican Queen*. With their navigation lights gleaming in the morning twilight, the two planes taxied out to the runway.

The *Silver Turtle* went first. The little plane made a short accelerating zoom along the runway and lifted up into the air, climbing steeply. Their increasing height lengthened Sam's view, and although it was still dark down on the ground, from up here he could see the orange ball of the sun appearing above the eastern horizon. Amy banked round onto a southeasterly course, and Sam squinted as the sun's amber rays hit his face. The sunlight gave little warmth against the chilly air rushing past him, but his spirits soared anyhow. They were on their way at last.

Sam heard the buzz of the *Silver Turtle*'s electric motors drop a little in pitch and guessed Amy was slowing the plane slightly to let Gabrielle catch up. He turned to look back and, sure enough, there was the *Pelican Queen*, roaring up on their port side. Sam waved to Zara, Ben and Adam, whom he could see in the *Pelican Queen*'s glazed cockpit, waving back.

The two planes levelled out at an altitude of six hundred metres. In side-by-side formation, they sped over the chalk cliffs of Kent and on over the sea to the wide world beyond.

8

The long journey to Southeast Asia was a fabulous one. Each morning, Gabrielle and Amy piloted the two flying boats for about four hours before landing for a lunch break at a prearranged location. Another four hours' flying each afternoon took them to their overnight stopover destinations. Flying at 250 miles per hour, this schedule enabled them to cover about two thousand miles each day. The two planes flew at a much lower height than jet airliners, giving an exhilarating and detailed view of the coastlines, landscapes, towns and cities they were passing over.

On the first day, they flew southeastwards across Europe on a course that included a breathtaking crossing of the snow-capped Austrian Alps, a lunch stop at the ancient Croatian port of Dubrovnik, and a lovely flight over the island-studded Aegean Sea. They landed for the night in Cyprus, where a friend of Professor Sharpe in the UN peacekeeping force looked after them, providing an evening meal and arranging to have the planes refuelled and recharged.

On day two, they crossed the Middle East, flying over Lebanon, Syria, Jordan and Saudi Arabia in the morning. The flight over these last two countries was a slight detour. The most direct route would have taken them over Iraq instead, but the ongoing conflict in that country ruled this option out as too dangerous. Most of the children's ideas about what the Middle East was like had been shaped by news reports of war and violence, but Professor Gauntraker pointed out that the region was one of the ancient world's cradles of civilisation, and he brought the countries alive for them with stories of their rich history and culture. He also described his own travels through this part of the world and, looking down over the vast, beautiful, wind-sculpted desert, the children could imagine a younger Professor Gauntraker traversing the sands by camel. After a lunch stop in Kuwait and a long afternoon flight down the Persian Gulf, they reached Muscat, the capital of Oman, by nightfall. Here, their host was a young sheikh whose father had been a travelling companion of Professor Gauntraker many years ago.

The morning of day three was spent crossing the Arabian Sea. They reached the west coast of India by lunchtime, landing for the pilots' break near Mumbai. Their afternoon flight took them right across southern central India, over an endlessly fascinating landscape of mountain ridges, wooded valleys, arid plains, wide rivers, rice paddy fields, little villages, sprawling towns and a few immense cities. They landed in the evening near the east coast city of Nellore, at an airfield where Gabrielle had once worked as a flying instructor.

The five children swapped between the two planes for the different stages of the trip. In the *Silver Turtle*, as promised, Amy gave each of them a few flying lessons in the co-pilot's seat, and they also took turns at riding in the nose hatch.

On the *Pelican Queen*, there were many fun places to sit – in a comfortable window seat in the lounge, up in the observation bubble in the tail, or in one of the seats in the glazed cockpit. Any child or adult who chose to sit in the co-pilot's seat was likely to find themselves being thrown into an impromptu flying lesson from Gabrielle, whether they'd asked for one or not. The *Pelican Queen*'s controls were more complicated and heavier to handle than those of the *Silver Turtle*, and Gabrielle's favourite teaching method – suddenly letting go of her controls completely and assisting her pupil only with a barrage of vocal instructions – made her flying lessons a good bit scarier than Amy's.

Marcia really took to flying. She soon became almost as proficient as Ben at piloting the *Silver Turtle* and was making good progress in the *Pelican Queen*, too. Gabrielle would have made her try some take-offs and landings, but (slightly to Marcia's relief) the other adults insisted that only the two proper pilots should do these during the expedition.

Sam loved being in either plane's cockpit, whether he was having a flying lesson or not. He enjoyed studying the array of instrument dials, learning how to read what they all meant and finding out how they all worked. During the journey, he got to know the inner workings of both the flying boats pretty well, and spent many happy moments helping Professor Ampersand with ongoing maintenance jobs and with a few little inventions.

Professor Ampersand's electric outboard motor (used with the inflatable boat for ferrying themselves to and from the flying boats) proved very successful – speedy and almost silent.

Professor Pottle's urine-powered combined-fan-and-insect-repeller wasn't quite so successful, though it added to the interest of the journey (as far as Oman, at least, where somehow Professor Gauntraker managed 'accidentally' to leave it behind).

Ben's favourite place to sit was at the navigator's desk in the *Pelican Queen*'s cockpit, just behind the pilots' seats. The desk was equipped with a compass and a drawer full of rulers, pencils and protractors – a purpose-built place for him to help work out their course for the day ahead, and to chart their ongoing progress on his foldable map of the world.

Zara was keeping a sketchbook journal of the expedition, filling the pages of a sturdily bound drawing pad with pictures of the places they stopped at and the places they flew over. She drew the pictures with a lovely old black ink pen that Professor Ampersand had given to her, and coloured some of them using a little tin of watercolours. Around and beneath her pictures she jotted down details about what they'd seen and done at each place, and about all the amazingly hospitable people they'd met.

Adam was also keeping a record of the expedition, taking dozens of pictures on a digital camera that Professor Sharpe had recently bought him. Marcia gently joked that Adam's photographic memory was so good, he'd hardly need actual photos to be able to recall the trip later, but Adam said that it was good to have images that he could share. Professor Gadling had brought along his laptop computer, which was rigged up with a satellite transmitter, so they were able to email Adam's pictures to Professor Sharpe, Professor Hartleigh-Broadbeam, Professor Pottle and Sam's parents.

On day four they crossed the Bay of Bengal, lunched by one of the Nicobar Islands, and traversed the Andaman Sea to reach the west coast of Peninsular Malaysia. Here, they flew over cities that were composed of a striking mixture of sleek ultramodern skyscrapers and sprawling ramshackle

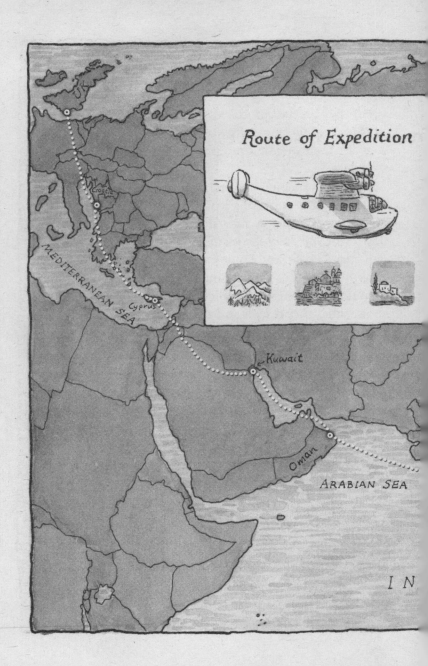

Route of Expedition

MEDITERRANEAN SEA

Cracow

Cyprus

Kuwait

Oman

ARABIAN SEA

I N

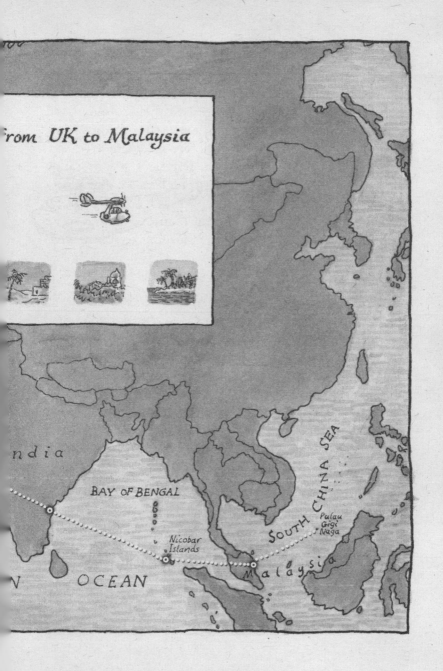

from UK to Malaysia

n d i a

BAY OF BENGAL

Nicobar
Islands

OCEAN

SOUTH CHINA SEA

Pulau
Gigi
Naga

M a l a y s i a

shanty-town areas. Then they flew up over the rolling green hills and forested mountains in the centre of the peninsula, reaching the east coast by late afternoon, where they made a brief stop at Kerteh airport to refuel and recharge the two aircraft, and to have their passports and other documents checked. From there, they made a short flight along the coast, and, just before sunset, the two aircraft touched down on the calm waters of a wide, sandy bay. The bay was a turtle sanctuary run by a Malaysian naturalist, Dr Shariman, whom Professor Sharpe knew through the World Wide Fund for Nature. This was to be their final overnight stop before heading to Pulau Gigi Naga.

Sam, sitting in the cockpit of the *Pelican Queen*, had his binoculars out and was looking at a large wooden bungalow at one end of the beach. It was the only building in the vicinity. Behind the beach was an area of palm trees and other tropical vegetation which, as they had seen from the air, formed a strip about half a kilometre wide between the coast and the nearest main road. The treetops were now silhouetted against the sunset. Although it was evening, the air was hot – hotter even than it had been in India or the Middle East, and considerably more humid.

The bungalow looked quite new, though was traditionally Malayan in style – built from wood with a wide veranda all around it, and raised above the ground on short stilts. In the fading light, Sam could just make out the lettering on a signboard: TELUK BATUKECIL TURTLE SANCTUARY. He could also see a motorboat setting off towards them from a low wooden jetty.

The boat was driven by a middle-aged Malayan man wearing a floral-print shirt. A young man sat next to him. Both men smiled and waved as they reached the two aircraft.

'Welcome to Teluk Batukecil,' hailed the middle-aged man. 'I am Dr Shariman Samsuddin. And this is Simon Arblinton. He arrived here shortly before you landed.'

'Really pleased to meet you guys at last,' said the young archaeologist. He was tall and slim, with pale skin and light-brown hair. He wore a fawn safari shirt, dusty brown trousers and a pair of delicate-looking wire-framed spectacles.

Dr Shariman guided the pilots to two anchored buoys where the flying boats could be moored for the night. The name of the smaller aircraft clearly delighted him. 'Our sanctuary has offered hospitality to several different species of turtle,' he said, as he and Simon helped to fasten the mooring lines. 'Green turtles, hawksbill turtles, leatherback turtles. But never before have we been honoured with a visit from a *silver* turtle.'

Everyone clambered into the boat and introduced themselves properly to Dr Shariman and to Simon.

'Did you have a good journey down from Thailand, Simon?' asked Professor Gadling.

'Yeah, no probs,' said Simon. 'Flight to Kuala Terengganu, bus down to Kuala Dungun, and one of Dr Shariman's guys was kind enough to pick me up from there in the sanctuary's jeep. I can't claim to have been travelling as stylishly as you, though,' he added. 'Your flying boats are seriously cool.'

Dr Shariman drove the craft back to the jetty, and told them a bit about his work on the way. 'The main purpose of our sanctuary', he explained, 'is to preserve this beach as a safe nesting site for the turtles. As you probably know, female turtles come ashore at night to lay their eggs and bury them in the sand. But many of their beaches have become too built-up with tourist developments – too many people, too many bright lights, too much noise. Even the tourists who come to see the turtles often frighten them away. And then there is the problem of the eggs being dug up, to be sold for human consumption. Sea turtles have been around for a hundred million years, yet now, thanks to human activity, they're threatened with extinction – like so many other creatures, as I'm sure you all know.'

'Yeah,' said Marcia sadly. 'Some scientists think that half of all the species that are around on earth today will go extinct in the next hundred years.'

'Well at least here, and at other sanctuaries, we are doing what we can to reverse that trend for turtles,' said Dr Shariman. 'During the nesting season, between April and September, we guard their nest sites, and bring some of the eggs into our incubators to improve their chances of hatching successfully. But our small efforts may not be enough.'

They arrived at the jetty, and Dr Shariman led everyone up to the bungalow, where they met his wife Suhana and the turtle sanctuary's three young employees. A long table on the front section of the veranda had been covered with a white cloth and set for dinner, and from somewhere inside the bungalow, appetising smells were wafting out into the sultry evening air.

Dr Shariman decided there was just time before dinner

for a quick tour of the sanctuary's laboratory at the back of the bungalow, and showed them several juvenile and adult turtles of various species living in large tanks. These were turtles that had been injured by speedboats or fishing nets and brought in to be cared for until they were well enough to be released back into the sea. Seeing these strange yet beautiful creatures close up, the children could understand why Dr Shariman and his team were dedicating themselves to trying to save them from extinction.

They returned to the veranda. It was quickly turning dark, and the first stars were appearing in the sky. As they were close to the equator, the setting of the sun and the change between day and night happened more rapidly than it did back home (an effect Professor Ampersand had explained to the children the previous evening, using a melon as a makeshift globe). In the trees behind the beach, the evening calls of birds gave way to an increase in insect noise, dominated by the cacophonous rhythmic chirruping of cicadas.

On the veranda, candles and paraffin lamps were lit, and everyone sat down to enjoy a delicious dinner of fish, meat, vegetable and rice dishes. As they ate, they watched a near-full moon rise above the sea, casting a silvery sheen over its calm surface.

Conversation first turned briefly to the expedition's destination. 'Professor Sharpe mentioned in her email that you're looking for early human remains on Pulau Gigi Naga,' said Dr Shariman. 'But she also explained that you're trying to keep the details of what you're hoping to discover secret until you find firm evidence, so don't worry – I won't pry any further. I'll simply wish you the best of luck. And I'm sure you'll find the island fascinating in any case. I've heard it's very beautiful.'

'It's surprising that people haven't tried to ruin the island,' said Marcia. 'To turn it into a tourist resort or something, or let logging companies into its forests.'

'Oh, there have been many such plans put forward over recent decades,' said Dr Shariman. 'But I've heard that the Malaysian government has always been persuaded by one of its most senior environmental advisers to keep the island as an uninhabited nature reserve. I have never met this adviser, but by all accounts, those of us working to save wildlife in this part of the world have much to thank him for.'

For the rest of dinner, everyone chatted sociably about all sorts of things. Amy and the children told Simon how they'd built the *Silver Turtle*, and Simon told everyone a bit about the excavations he'd been working on in Thailand. The young archaeologist had a pleasant, easy-going manner, and by the end of the meal, he seemed very much part of the expedition group.

Wilfred sat beaming as he soaked up the lively, good-natured atmosphere. His face had worn a similar expression of carefree enthusiasm throughout the whole journey from Britain. He was a very different person from the nervous, uptight man who had introduced himself three weeks earlier.

'Well,' said Professor Ampersand, at about quarter-past ten. 'If we're wanting to set out for Gigi Naga reasonably early tomorrow morning, maybe we should think about getting back to the *Pelican Queen* for an early night.' He leaned back in his cane chair and gave a yawning stretch.

'I'll take you back in the boat,' said Dr Shariman, getting

to his feet.

'Oh, I'll need to get my rucksack,' said Simon. 'It's still in the back of your jeep.' He headed off round to the back of the bungalow, where the sanctuary's vehicles were parked. While they were waiting for him, the rest of the group thanked their hosts for their splendid hospitality and food.

'It has been our pleasure,' said Suhana. 'Will you come and have an early breakfast with us tomorrow before you leave?'

But before anyone could answer, a chilling sound cut through the night air — a sudden cry of alarm and pain, coming from somewhere behind the bungalow.

10

A second after it had started, the cry ended abruptly in a strangulated croak. Adam was the first to respond, springing from his chair and tearing off around the side of the veranda at lightning speed. Zara, Ben, Sam, Marcia, Amy and the three young sanctuary employees were close on his heels, followed by the seven older adults.

They rounded the corner at the back of the bungalow. The dusty car park was unlit, but in the moonlight Zara could make out Simon − recognisable by his pale shirt − being violently attacked by three darkly clad figures, whose heads were covered by black, ninja-style masks. One assailant was holding Simon from behind with an arm round his throat; the other two were grappling and punching him from the front. Simon was attempting to fend them off with flailing kicks, but was clearly badly outnumbered.

'Leave him alone!' yelled Adam, bravely leading the mass charge across the car park. He was about to reach the fray and, for a moment, Zara was terrified the attackers might turn on him. But the three figures − presumably seeing that the small boy was backed up by fifteen other people − released Simon and fled into the black shadows of the trees and bushes.

As the five children and Amy started to pursue the

attackers, the sanctuary employees overtook them. 'Stay at the bungalow!' shouted one of them. 'Don't put yourselves in danger. Leave it to us!'

'He is right,' said Dr Shariman, panting as he caught up. 'You will get lost in the dark undergrowth and instead of catching those men you may be attacked by them yourselves. My employees know the paths well and will keep together. Come on; we must see to Simon.'

They returned to find Simon leaning against the front of the jeep, already being looked after by the other adults. He was bruised and battered, with a sore neck and a bleeding nose, but a check of his limbs and ribs established that he hadn't suffered any substantial injuries. Adam noticed that his glasses had been knocked off and spotted them on the ground. Luckily, they weren't broken.

'Thanks,' croaked Simon, putting them back on. 'I was wondering why everything looked blurry.' He attempted a groggy smile, though his voice wavered and he was obviously badly shaken.

'Carry him into the bungalow where he can lie down,' said Suhana.

'Don't need to lie down,' insisted Simon. 'Just . . . just let me sit down for ten minutes and I'll be fine. Could somebody carry my rucksack?'

As Marcia turned to lift the rucksack from the back of the jeep, her foot kicked against something. She stooped to see what the object was and gasped. 'Look at this!' she said to the others. Sam took out the tiny but powerful keyring torch that he always carried in a pocket and shone it where she pointed. There, sticking into the dusty ground, was a small knife, part of its lethal-looking blade still visible.

'One of those men almost stabbed me with

it,' said Simon, wincing as he bent to pull the knife out of the earth. 'But I managed to kick it out of his hand.'

'There might be fingerprints on the handle,' said Adam. 'We shouldn't touch it until the police can look at it, should we?'

'You're right,' said Simon, quickly handing the weapon to Dr Shariman, who had his handkerchief out ready to take it. 'Hope I haven't smudged any prints that were there. I wasn't thinking straight.'

'You can hardly be blamed for that after what you've been through!' said Dr Shariman. 'Come on, let's get you a seat and a cup of hot sweet tea.'

They helped Simon walk back round to the front of the bungalow, where he flopped down in one of the veranda chairs.

'Now, can you tell us what happened?' asked Dr Shariman, once the tea had been brought and sipped.

'I'd got round to the car park and was just approaching the jeep, when I heard a noise that made me turn round,' said Simon, beginning to sound less shaky. 'I saw those three men trying to climb in through one of the windows at the back of the bungalow. They saw me and instantly rushed over to attack me. Guess they wanted to put me out of action so they could carry on with their robbery. They must have been after turtle eggs from your incubators.'

'Hmm, maybe,' said Dr Shariman. 'But if those men were involved in the illegal trade in turtle eggs, you would expect them to know they would not find any this late in the year. And in any case, it would be unusual for people who take turtle eggs to go to such lengths as breaking into a building, or attacking anyone.'

'It is more likely that these men were trying to steal our

office computer,' said Suhana, 'or things from our living quarters. I have a little jewellery. But no one has ever tried to rob us before. Crime – especially violent crime – is unusual round here.'

'Perhaps the thieves saw our planes landing earlier', suggested Gabrielle, 'and assumed that we were rich tourists who were staying at the bungalow, with loads of expensive cameras and watches and stuff for them ter nick.'

Ben shuddered, his eyes drawn to the razor-sharp knife, which had been placed on the table.

'Well, they must have underestimated how many of us there are,' said Zara, noticing her brother's unease and hiding her own. 'They ran off pretty quickly when we challenged them.'

'Absolutely,' said Professor Ampersand, firmly. 'I'm sure they won't come back now.'

'Even so, this is very worrying,' said Dr Shariman. 'Can you describe the men, Simon?'

'I'm afraid I can't,' said Simon. 'Their faces were completely covered by those balaclava things.'

The three sanctuary employees returned, to report that their pursuit had been unsuccessful. The intruders had bolted into the thickest vegetation, avoiding any of the paths, and had vanished in the darkness without trace or sound.

Dr Shariman telephoned the police, who sent out two officers in a car from the nearest town, several miles away. The policemen were very concerned that violent burglars were operating in what was generally a region of low crime. They examined the knife and found it was a flick-knife, with a button on the handle to make the blade spring out or to enable it to be slid back in. After taking Simon's fingerprints, to differentiate his from any others they might find on the handle, they took the knife away for further scrutiny, promising to return in the morning to check for footprints in the car park and fingerprints at the bungalow window.

'I'm so sorry your stay here has been ruined by all this,' said Dr Shariman, after the police had driven off.

'Maybe your expedition's departure to Pulau Gigi Naga should be delayed for a day,' suggested Suhana, 'so that Simon can rest tomorrow.'

'That's if Simon even wants to continue with us after this,' said Wilfred. His old air of pessimism was beginning to return.

But Simon was having none of such talk. 'We can't let the brainless activities of three burglars put a downer on everything,' he insisted. 'No harm's been done, and at least we stopped them breaking in and stealing anything. We're all psyched up for getting to Gigi Naga tomorrow and we should stick to our plans. Let me get a good night's sleep, and I'll be fit for anything.'

'Good lad,' said Professor Gauntraker. 'If Simon's not going to let this incident spoil our stay here, none of us should. And *you*'ve certainly nothing to be sorry for, Dr Shariman.'

The others all added their heartfelt agreement to these sentiments.

'You are all very kind and brave,' said Dr Shariman. 'And you need not worry about those burglars coming back. My staff and I will stay up to keep a watch over your planes and the bungalow. It's no trouble. We are used to staying up all night during the turtles' nesting season anyway. Now, shall I ferry you all back to your flying boat before your planned early night gets any later?'

Soon, the expedition group was back on board the *Pelican*

Queen, where Simon was shown his bedroom cabin. He was also shown the skull and the moth-wing carving from Wilfred's biscuit tin. 'Mind-blowing!' he declared, after studying both objects very closely for several moments. 'I can't wait to get to that cave!' The young archaeologist's resolutely upbeat attitude was infectious, and as everyone got ready for bed, there was much excited talk about their plans for tomorrow.

Adam, though, seemed rather quiet and introverted as he got into his camp-bed, and Sam and Ben reassured him that they were quite safe now.

'It's all right,' said Adam, snapping out of his reverie. 'I wasn't worrying; I was just trying to puzzle something out. But it isn't important.'

Ben was in the lower bunk in the boys' cabin, beside the open porthole. He looked out over the moonlit sea. He could see quite a few distant lights, but these, he knew, were only the lights of ships. There was no land between here and Pulau Gigi Naga — nothing but six hundred miles of water. He imagined looking way, way beyond the horizon, imagined the island as it would be right now — totally wild and remote, totally dark except for moonlight, waiting to be explored by them.

The girls' cabin porthole was facing the shore. As Zara turned off the light and started closing the curtains, she could see the lamps burning on the bungalow's veranda, and could make out the figures of Dr Shariman and one of his men keeping their all-night vigil, armed with long, stout sticks. The other two employees, she knew, were guarding the back of the building. Everything was safe now, she told herself. The thieves would not come back. They had run away when challenged. Yet, as she drifted off to sleep, it was not the image of the masked intruders fleeing that kept replaying in her memory; it was the image of them attacking Simon, with such raw, vehement aggression.

11

The rest of the night passed uneventfully. Early the next morning, as arranged, Dr Shariman came to ferry them ashore for breakfast. He had also arranged for a local market trader to call by the sanctuary in his van, so that the expedition could stock up with fruit, vegetables, nuts, bread and rice to supplement their tinned supplies during the coming days.

While they were making the necessary purchases, the police returned. But they didn't have much to report. No one they'd spoken to at any of the local villages had seen any suspicious strangers in the vicinity. And the only fingerprints that had been found on the knife handle were those that had been left by Simon.

'The guy wielding it may have been wearing gloves,' said Simon. 'It was hard to tell in the dark, with everything happening so quickly.'

The policemen checked the window frame, but no prints were found there either, which further supported the theory that the intruders had indeed been gloved. No footprints were found in the stony ground by the window. All the police could really do was promise that their cars would make regular patrols in the area for the next few nights, and advise Dr Shariman to make his windows more secure.

By 9.30 a.m, with their food bought, their water containers filled and their thanks given, the expedition was ready for departure. The two aircraft left the water together and soared up into the clear blue sky.

The flight seemed to pass quickly. The fact that they were on the last leg of their journey – finally about to reach their destination – created an air of light-headed anticipation on board the two aircraft.

Once the coast of Peninsular Malaysia had vanished behind them, there was no land visible in any direction; just the wide expanse of the South China Sea. The sea was not empty though. They saw many ships – huge cargo vessels stacked with metal containers, and long oil tankers – and they flew over quite a few oil rigs and gas-drilling platforms.

'They've found a lot of oil and gas beneath the South China Sea in recent decades,' commented Professor Gadling, who was sitting in the *Pelican Queen's* lounge with Zara, Marcia and Simon. 'And it's believed there's a lot more to be found yet. It's led to some bitter territorial disputes between the different countries of this region, particularly over the ownership of the Spratly Islands, a widely scattered group of tiny reefs and atolls lying some way to the northeast of Pulau Gigi Naga.'

'Why do people always have to fight over everything?' said Marcia disdainfully. 'In every part of the world we've flown over, people are having wars, or wrecking the environment, or both.'

'Well, yeah,' said Zara, 'but in every part of the world where we've landed, we've met really *good* people – people who are trying to make things better.' Much as Zara admired Marcia's commitment to environmental causes, she found her constantly negative view of the human race too one-sided.

After about two-and-a-quarter hours' flying time had elapsed, Gabrielle announced that they should be able to see Pulau Gigi Naga soon. Everyone who had been in the *Pelican Queen*'s lounge went forward to stand behind the seats in the cockpit for a better forward view. On the *Silver Turtle* also, everyone stared intently ahead.

Suddenly, several people on both planes shouted 'There!' simultaneously. A very faint and very small grey-blue smudge had materialised on the horizon.

Gradually, the island began to look more distinct in shape and greener in colour. 'That's Pulau Gigi Naga all right,' said Wilfred, who was sitting behind Gabrielle. 'You can see the outline of the dragon's-teeth crags now.'

The planes lost height as they approached. Ben was in the *Silver Turtle*'s nose hatch and, from this perfect view-point, he gazed at the island – the island that he had been imagining in his head for the past three-and-a-half weeks, ever since Wilfred had first shown them his map. Ben had found that in life sometimes things you'd been looking forward to for ages didn't quite live up to your expectations in reality, but this wasn't the case now. Pulau Gigi Naga looked even more exciting and beautiful and mysterious and exotic than he'd dared to hope.

It also looked larger than Ben had been envisaging. On their small-scale maps of Southeast Asia, Pulau Gigi Naga featured as a mere speck, especially compared to the region's many huge islands, and because of this Ben had grown used to thinking of it as really tiny. But an island seven miles long and four miles wide is quite a substantial piece of land when you see it for real.

As proposed by Professor Gauntraker when they'd first looked at Wilfred's map, the two planes were aiming for the bay that formed the middle of Gigi Naga's west coast. The coastline to either side of the bay consisted of steep cliffs, which had been carved by the sea over thousands of years into some fabulous rock formations – dramatic overhangs that seemed to defy gravity; lofty sea-stack pillars that looked equally precarious; and elegant stone arches whose undersides glowed with shimmering patterns of sunlight bouncing off the waves below.

The bay itself was sandy. The sand was smooth and pristine – a dazzling white above the shoreline and a deepening turquoise where it sloped away beneath the sea.

The back of the beach was fringed by palms and other tropical trees and shrubs, which formed the edge of the island's rainforest. The island's terrain sloped steeply upwards from the coast into a cluster of tall hills near the centre. The lush, green forest cloaked this landscape almost completely. Only the twelve towering rocky 'teeth' that formed the summits of the hills were treeless.

The two planes touched down in the bay, and the pilots brought them to rest a few hundred metres from the beach. As the noise of the engines and motors ceased, Zara just sat gazing at the island without speaking, listening to the sounds reaching them across the water – the gentle crash of small waves breaking on the shore; the squawks, whistles and strange, echoing whoops of forest birds and animals. After a few seconds, Zara noticed that everyone else in the cockpit was also remaining still and silent while they took in these first impressions of Pulau Gigi Naga. No one had *suggested* that they should do so; the island just seemed to have had that effect on them. It had something to do with the fact that the island was uninhabited, Zara thought. It felt as if they were pausing at the edge of another world – a world where nature went about its business without any human involvement; a world they could enter respectfully, but one in which they didn't really belong.

'Well,' said Gabrielle at last. 'We got here.'

'We did indeed,' said Professor Gadling. 'Well done, pilots! Now, let's get the *Pelican Queen* anchored, get ourselves organised, and get the first lot of people and equipment transferred to the *Silver Turtle*. The sooner we're all up at the lake, the sooner we can find Wilfred's cave – and whatever's inside it.'

12

Everyone worked quickly. Sam clambered into the compartment in the *Pelican Queen*'s bows where her mooring equipment was stowed, and lowered the anchor (a job he had learned to do pretty speedily during the journey out).

Zara and Marcia helped Professor Ampersand to inflate the rubber boat and attach his electric outboard motor. The boat would be needed to transfer equipment and people from the *Pelican Queen* to the *Silver Turtle*.

Simon helped Professor Gauntraker select the items of archaeology equipment from the cargo hold that were most likely to be useful in making their initial exploration of the cave – pickaxes and shovels, as well as much smaller trowels and scrapers for careful digging.

Professor Gauntraker also unpacked ropes, torches, water bottles and the three machetes. Then he made sure that everyone had properly covered their skin with sun cream and insect repellent, had liberally sprinkled the inside of their socks with fungicide and anti-leech powder, and had changed into their sturdy jungle trousers and trekking boots. 'Nothing will *totally* prevent the leeches and insects from getting you,' he said (with some relish, Ben thought), 'but these precautions should at least discourage some of 'em.'

Three trips would be necessary for Amy to fly everyone

up to the lake, and it was decided that the first group should be made up of Wilfred, Professor Gauntraker and two of the children. The children drew straws for these places, and Zara and Adam won, but Ben, Marcia and Sam didn't mind. They'd be going on the second run, only a few minutes after the first.

With the first group aboard, Amy started the *Silver Turtle*'s motors and took off. The little plane zoomed over the beach and on over the rainforest, up towards the craggy summits of the island's central hills. They looked down onto the forest treetops, an irregular canopy of green, with occasional splashes of other colours where a tree had come into flower. Adam, sitting in the nose–hatch seat, pointed to a trio of large birds flapping slowly over the forest canopy on broad black wings. The tops of their massive beaks looked like bizarrely misshapen red–and–yellow chilli peppers, and Professor Gauntraker identified the birds as rhinoceros hornbills.

They reached the 'dragon's teeth' and, following Wilfred's map, Amy piloted a course between two of these strange, angular peaks. From this relatively close distance, Zara could see that even these rocky crags were not entirely devoid of plant life. Here and there, ferns and trailing vines were growing from narrow ledges and cracks. Clearly this was an environment in which nature managed to thrive everywhere.

The terrain between the two hills formed a shallow, densely forested valley, and there, coming into view in the valley's centre, was an oval of water.

'That's the lake, all right,' said Wilfred. 'It looks even smaller than I remember it, though. Will you have room to land?'

'It's aboot the size I was expecting from your map,' said

Amy, 'though it's going tae be tricky tae come in low enough with all the trees aroond it. But I'll give it a shot.' She reduced their speed and altitude. 'I'll make a low pass over the water first tae check for obstacles,' she said. 'Everyone keep their eyes peeled – especially you, Adam. You've got the best view.' She spoke loudly to make sure Adam could hear her above the buzz of the motors.

In a manoeuvre that made Zara's stomach lurch, Amy swooped the *Silver Turtle* down over the lakeside trees, then levelled out to fly along the length of the lake with the aircraft's hull just a metre above the water. Everyone peered hard, their eyes searching for rocks or logs that might be protruding from the surface or lying just beneath it. The water was greeny-brown, but clear enough to see into.

'It looks free of obstructions to me,' reported Adam, and the others concurred.

'Good,' said Amy. Just as Zara was beginning to worry that they might crash into the trees at the other end of the lake, Amy yanked back her control column and sent the *Silver Turtle* soaring up over them. Then she banked the plane through a tight U-turn, descended back the way they'd just come, and this time landed on the water. With the motors cut, the aircraft came to a halt before it reached the end of the lake, but without much room to spare.

'Good work, Amy,' said Professor Gauntraker.

'Nae problem,' said Amy. 'How does it feel tae be back here, Wilfred?'

'Strange,' said Wilfred, 'but in a good way. I never managed to appreciate how beautiful all this was when I was here with the army, being bawled at all the time by the captain.'

The little lake was indeed a beautiful spot. One side consisted of a bank of rock, a few metres high in places, which had several small waterfalls cascading down it into the lake from the forested hillside above. The other side had a beach of silt and shingle, and at one end, some big, flat rocks. Here, the water flowed out from the lake and into a small river. The river was marked on Wilfred's map, which showed that it meandered down through the rainforest to reach the sea at an inlet on the island's northern coast.

The varied calls and chatterings of wildlife could be heard from the forest all around them, though the only animals that Zara could actually see were insects – dragonflies hovering over the lake, orange butterflies fluttering around a flowering bush, and various sorts of flies buzzing about everywhere in the hot, humid air. As the *Silver Turtle* had come into land, Zara had seen a brown, long-necked bird fly up from the water and into the trees, and she guessed that their arrival must have scared other creatures around the lake into hiding, too.

Now that they were actually on the island, surrounded by ancient rainforest with no view of the sea below, Zara's sense of entering a domain where they didn't belong was even stronger than it had been down in the bay. Gazing around the undergrowth and foliage, she had the distinct feeling that their intrusion into this island world was being watched by dozens of unseen birds, reptiles and mammals. Even the twelve towering crags seemed to be looking down on them, like giant stone sentinels. It wasn't an unpleasant feeling, but it was a rather strange one.

'If you taxi us over to those shallows, Amy,' said Professor Gauntraker, pointing to the shingly edge, 'we can wade ashore. Would that put us on the right side of the lake to get to the cave, Wilfred?'

'Er, yes,' said Wilfred. 'Everything's a bit different to how I remember it, but I reckon that must be the bit of shore I was standing on when I first noticed the cave.'

Soon Zara, Adam, Wilfred and Professor Gauntraker were ashore, with the batch of equipment they had brought stacked on the flat rocks.

'We'll see if Wilfred can spot the cave again by the time you've got everyone up here,' called Professor Gauntraker to Amy as she taxied back to the end of the lake to start her take-off.

'But we promise we won't go and look at it till everyone's here,' added Zara.

They watched Amy go, relieved to see the *Silver Turtle* safely clear the treetops once more.

Wilfred stood at the water's edge and turned to scan the rainforest behind him. The others followed his gaze, but the vegetation was so dense and tangly that it was impossible to see any distance into the forest. Wilfred paced back and forth along the shingle, continuing to peer into the foliage, trying in vain to find a gap through which to see clearly. 'I'm almost certain this is where I was standing when I spotted the cave,' said Wilfred, 'but back then I had a clearish view through the trees and bushes. That's why I could see the rock-face, even though it was a couple of hundred yards away.'

'Then this bit of forest must have grown bushier in the last fifty years,' said Zara.

'You're right,' said Wilfred, looking worried. 'I was stupid to assume that everything would be the same after all this time. And these plants aren't only blocking our *view* into the rainforest; they're blocking our way, too. I'm really sorry. It's not going to be as easy to find the cave as I thought.'

'Don't worry,' said Professor Gauntraker. 'I certainly wasn't assuming it would be easy. That's why I brought these.' He unsheathed one of the three machetes. 'We should be able to hack a way through. It'll be tough, unpleasant work, mind.' His voice was sombre but, from the gleam in his eye, Zara could tell he was actually delighted that they had this extra difficulty to overcome and a reason to use these dangerous-looking expedition tools. 'We'd better wait for the others before starting into the jungle,' he said. 'We may as well eat our lunch rations. We'll sit in that patch of shade by the equipment. But keep a close eye on the lake. There could be crocodiles here.'

No one saw any crocodiles, though they saw plenty of fish and quite a few frogs.

Within a fairly short space of time, Amy had brought everyone else up to the lake – first Sam, Ben, Marcia and Professor Gadling; then, making up the last group, Professor Ampersand, Gabrielle and Simon. Sam helped Amy hitch the *Silver Turtle* securely to a lakeside tree by the mooring rope.

The equipment brought by all three trips made quite a pile on the rocks. 'We can leave most of that here until we find the cave,' said Professor Gauntraker. 'Once we've hacked ourselves a path, it won't take us long to come back for what we need. Now, let's get started. Which direction should we head in, Wilfred?'

'Er, that way, I think,' said Wilfred, pointing into the dense vegetation, 'though I might be remembering it wrong after fifty years.'

Professor Gauntraker wielded one of the machetes himself, and gave another to Simon. The third he told the children to take turns with. Their course took them uphill as they headed away from the lakeside, and the ground was soft – a mixture of mud and rotting leaves. With the prickly bushes to fight through and the sweltering sauna-like heat, it was hard going, but none of the children minded. Ben breathed in the rainforest's warm, damp, planty smell and grinned at Sam as he brushed a large ant from his arm. This was the kind of exploring of which he'd always dreamed.

As they slowly made progress, Professor Gauntraker gave the children lessons in machete technique. 'This type of machete is a traditional Malayan design called a parang,' he said, demonstrating the most efficient slashing motion. 'Specially built for cutting through this particularly woody vegetation you find in Southeast Asian jungle.'

His use of the word jungle reminded Zara of something she'd been wondering about for a while. 'Do jungle and rainforest mean the same thing?' she asked. 'Old films and books always seem to use the word jungle, but TV nature programmes seem to use the word rainforest.'

'Interesting point,' said Gabrielle. '*I've* noticed that people use the word rainforest when they're describing it as a beautiful, vulnerable place that needs saving, and use the word jungle when they're describing it as a hostile place that needs ter be defeated. Says a lot about the different ways we view the natural world.'

'Then we should definitely use the word rainforest,' said Marcia. 'The natural world needs protecting from *us* way more than *we* need protecting from *it*.'

'The natural world's quite capable of being hostile at the same time as being beautiful and vulnerable,' growled Professor Gauntraker, hacking at a particularly resistant and extremely thorny bush. 'Nature-lovers who live in modern cities have the luxury of forgetting that. Do you know how many people in the developing world die of snakebites?'

'Snakes should be protected!' said Marcia. 'I bet they kill hardly any people.'

'More than a hundred thousand each year!' insisted Professor Gauntraker.

'To return to Zara's question,' said Professor Gadling, 'it's actually only correct to use the word jungle for a particular *type* of rainforest vegetation – the sort of dense, tangled, low-growing stuff that we're fighting through now. Once we get deeper into the forest, where the high tree canopy blocks out most of the sunlight, you'll see that relatively little ground-level vegetation grows between the tree trunks. And it would be incorrect to refer to *that* sort of rainforest as jungle.'

'Hrmmph,' grunted Professor Gauntraker. 'You naturalists just like to keep changing the so-called correct words for everything so that you can lecture the rest of us. Jungle's always been a perfectly good general term, for those of us who've spent a lifetime actually exploring it.'

'Eric, you're not the *only* one who's spent a lifetime exploring rainforests,' snapped Professor Gadling. 'Some of us like to be reasonably knowledgeable about the habitats we're exploring, that's all.'

'*Reasonably knowledgeable?*' echoed Professor Gauntraker.

'Garrulous, I've more knowledge in my little finger than you have in your entire fat head. *Real* knowledge, that I've acquired from real experience of—'

'Hey!' said Ben. 'I think I can see some rocks ahead.'

For the past few minutes it had been Ben's turn with the third parang. Ignoring the professors' squabble, he had got on with the task of hacking through the tangle of plant life and had even overtaken Simon. Now Ben had emerged into the shadier interior of the rainforest where, as Professor Gadling had predicted, there was less undergrowth, and the view through the trees was a bit clearer.

Everyone caught up with Ben and saw what he had spotted: an almost vertical bank of dark rock forming part of the steepening hillside ahead of them, less than a hundred metres away. And at the base of the rock-face, a black, roughly triangular opening could be seen.

'That's it,' said Wilfred. 'That's the cave.'

13

Everyone hurried between the trees, up the sloping ground towards the rock-face and the cave.

'Well done, Wilfred,' said Amy, assisting him over a patch of particularly uneven ground. 'Your course intae the rain-forest was bang on.'

'Well, close enough, anyway,' said Wilfred. 'But I wish Professor Gauntraker and Professor Gadling hadn't fallen out with each other.' He cast a worried look at the two professors, who were a little way ahead.

'They haven't fallen out with each other!' Zara reassured him. 'They *like* arguing. And they won't even remember they've *had* an argument now that we've found your cave.'

The group reached the rock-face and everyone stood in silence for a moment as they peered into the blackness of the cave.

'You go first, Wilfred,' said Professor Ampersand. Wilfred led the way.

The mouth of the cave was not very wide or high, but once inside, as their eyes became accustomed to the gloom, they found that the cave itself was quite roomy. However, just as Wilfred had described, it was partly filled with the stones and boulders from a rockfall, some covering the ground, others forming a high heap which blocked up the back of the cave completely. Everyone's eyes were focused on the cave floor, looking for bones. But no one could see any.

'Er, whereabouts exactly is this skeleton half-buried, Wilfred?' asked Professor Gadling.

'I would have sworn it was round about here,' said Wilfred, pointing to the middle of the cave, where the rock debris was heaped a good half-metre high. 'I don't understand why we can't see any bones.'

Sam brought out his keyring torch and scanned the rubble with its narrow beam. But still no bones could be seen.

'I don't understand,' repeated Wilfred. 'Maybe I'm misremembering the *exact* spot but, like I said, some of the bones were clearly visible when I found the skeleton, and I didn't even have a torch back then. And the skeleton was almost *all* exposed by the time I'd shifted some rocks away.'

'You didn't cover the skeleton back over before you left?' asked Marcia.

'No,' said Wilfred. 'The captain was impatient for us to move on, remember. I only just had time to get the skull.'

'Er . . . you *have* brought us ter the right cave, Wilfred?' asked Gabrielle tentatively. 'It was fifty years ago, so no one'd blame you if this is a different cave, that you've mistaken for the one you were in back then.'

'That's *possible*,' admitted Wilfred. 'But I don't think so. Apart from the lack of the skeleton, this place seems so familiar.'

'Hmm, I suppose some animal could have taken the bones during the past fifty years,' said Professor Gadling. 'But I'm not sure how likely it is that any animal would bother with such old bones.'

'No,' agreed Simon, frowning, 'and it seems unlikely that a whole skeleton would be removed that way.'

Simon sounded worried, Zara noticed, his usual confident

manner thrown. Was he beginning to think he'd been dragged into a wild goose chase? Was he having doubts about the reliability of Wilfred's story? For a moment, Zara found herself having such doubts herself. What if there had never been a skeleton in the cave in the first place? What if, over the decades, Wilfred had elaborated his own memories of what he'd found in the cave, until he believed he remembered finding something that had never existed?

Zara tried to dismiss these thoughts as unfair and illogical. The skull was real enough, surely. Wilfred couldn't have faked something so convincing, could he? It seemed unlikely. But why was there no skeleton here?

An idea occurred to Sam. 'What if there's been another rockfall from the cave ceiling since Wilfred was last here,' he suggested, 'which has covered the skeleton up?' He shone his torch up to the cave ceiling, six or seven metres above them. The ceiling was rugged, its surface broken up by gaping black crevices edged by unstable-looking spurs of rock.

'I couldn't tell you whether more of the ceiling's come down since I was here before,' said Wilfred, looking up. 'I didn't have a torch back then, so I never had a proper look at it. But it seems possible. Earthquakes are fairly common in this part of the world.'

'Yeah, good thinking, Sam,' said Marcia. 'Let's try shifting this top layer of rubble.' She crouched down and started lifting some of the smaller rocks with her hands, flinging them away to the edge of the cave.

Everyone quickly joined in, concentrating their efforts on the place where Wilfred remembered the skeleton being. The biggest rocks were too heavy to lift easily, even with several pairs of hands, and they tended to be block-shaped rather than round, which meant they weren't easy to roll away, either. However, many of the rocks were small enough to be cleared without too much difficulty.

After they'd been working for a few minutes, Marcia suddenly spotted something beneath the rock she was removing. 'That looks like a bit of bone!' she exclaimed. Everyone looked at where she was pointing and Sam directed his torch beam. Sure enough, one end of a thin grey bone was protruding from the rocks beneath the one Marcia had just lifted away.

Everyone gave a spontaneous whooping cheer.

'Fantastic!' said Simon, his old air of upbeat enthusiasm restored.

'Sorry for questioning the reliability of your memory, Wilfred,' said Gabrielle. 'Looks like you've brought us tcr the right cave all right.'

Everyone quickly started lifting away the stones directly around Marcia's find, none more eagerly than Wilfred. Even in the gloom of the cave, Zara could see how happy Wilfred looked, now that his dream of mounting an expedition and rediscovering the skeleton had finally been fulfilled. She felt slightly ashamed for having momentarily doubted his story.

'Looks like an upper arm bone,' said Professor Gadling, a guess that was confirmed as correct as a shoulder joint was revealed, then part of the skeleton's ribcage.

'A lot more of these ribs are broken than they were when I found it before,' said Wilfrcd. 'It looks like the skeleton was badly crushed by the most recent rockfall. We'd better be careful how we uncover it. We don't want to break more of the bones, or lose any bits.'

'Yeah, you're right,' said Simon. 'We should zip back to the lake and fetch the proper gear before we uncover any more of it. We'll need a lamp or two so we can see what we're doing, the pickaxes to lever away the bigger boulders, and the fine scraper tools in case some of the bones are buried in the earth beneath these rocks. C'mon.'

Now that they knew the route and had a pathway cleared, it didn't take very long to get back to the lakeside and then return to the cave with the equipment they needed.

'We need a good overhead light to work by,' said Simon. 'I'll try to hang this lamp up here.' He clambered up onto the heap of boulders that blocked the back of the cave, carrying the largest hurricane lamp and an old tree branch. He wedged the branch firmly between the highest boulders so that it protruded by a good half-metre. Then he lit the lamp and hung it from the branch's end, from where it cast its light very effectively over the cave below.

'That's great, Simon,' said Amy.

'Can you see if the cave once went back any further?' asked Sam, noticing that Simon was lingering up near the top of the boulder heap and peering through the dark gaps between stones.

'Can't really tell,' said Simon. 'If it did, it's totally blocked off now. This rubble looks pretty solid.'

Simon came down and supervised the careful removal of rocks from the rest of the skeleton. With the leverage of the pickaxes, it was possible to lift the largest rocks and roll them to the edges of the cave. While half the group were doing this, the others continued to remove the smaller stones by hand. Adam had remembered to bring his camera, and took a photographic record of each stage of the uncovering process.

They worked quite slowly, party because it was hard work shifting the biggest boulders in the sweltering heat, and partly because even the smallest stones had to be lifted away very carefully to avoid risking further damage to the skeleton beneath.

At last, though, the entire skeleton lay revealed. Some bones were broken, some were out of position, and some were partly embedded in the earth of the cave floor, but in spite of this, the skeleton looked to be more or less complete – apart from the skull, of course, which was still in Wilfred's biscuit tin on board the *Pelican Queen*.

'It's every bit as extraordinary as you promised, Wilfred,' said Professor Gadling, crouching over the skeleton for a close inspection. 'Like you said, these arm bones are considerably longer than those of any *Homo sapiens* skeleton, and rather slimmer, too. In fact, that slender quality applies to most of the bones, wouldn't you say? I think our evolutionary cousin must have had a rather lightweight, gracile build, compared to our own.'

Everyone continued to examine and discuss the skeleton, while Adam photographed it from every angle.

'We should bring the skull with us tomorrow,' suggested Sam, 'so we can put it back with the skeleton, and photograph the whole thing together.'

'You're right,' agreed Professor Gauntraker. 'It'd enable us to show the experts how the skeleton was when Wilfred first found it.'

Zara looked down at the strange skeleton and envisaged how it would look with its even stranger skull back in place. She found herself trying to imagine what this individual had been like when it was alive, five thousand years ago. Had this one been a man or a woman? Had it lived in this cave? Had it sat round a fire here, part of a family group, chatting and laughing? Or had this species of human lived and behaved entirely differently from *Homo sapiens*?

Then suddenly, Zara's eyes spotted something half-embedded in the earth, near to the skeleton. It wasn't a piece of bone; it was too black for that. Jet-black. She crouched down and carefully began extracting the object from the ground, scraping the caked mud off its hard surfaces.

'What have you found, Zara?' asked Ben.

'Look,' she said, and held up the object: a piece of black, shiny jet, intricately carved into the form of a Malaysian moon moth, whose body and right wings were intact, but whose left wings were missing.

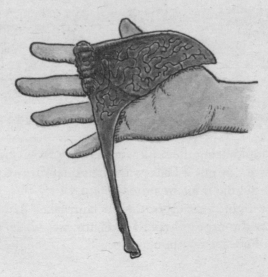

14

'The other half of Wilfred's moon moth carving!' exclaimed Marcia.

Everyone gathered round for a closer look. The head and body of the moth were as finely carved as the wings, and remarkably detailed.

'Have you got your bit with you, Wilfred?' asked Zara. 'So we can check that it joins together?'

'No, it's in the biscuit tin in my cabin on the *Pelican Queen*, with the skull,' said Wilfred, 'but I'm pretty sure that my bit *must* be the missing half of this.'

'Yes, I don't think there can be much doubt of that,' agreed Professor Gadling. 'Well done Zara for finding it.'

'Yeah,' said Simon. 'You guys are seriously good at spotting stuff. First the skeleton and now this.'

'So what's the plan now?' asked Gabrielle. 'Should we make a start on clearing the rocks from the rest of the cave floor? There could be other skeletons and more artefacts waiting ter be found.'

'Absolutely,' said Simon, 'though I don't know how much more we'll be able to get done before we have to stop for the day. I know it's only four-thirty, but we don't want to overdo it, especially in this heat.' He winced slightly and rubbed his ribs. 'I'm happy to bash on for a bit if everyone wants to, though,' he said.

'No,' said Professor Gadling, 'I think we should call it a day now and come back to it fresh in the morning. We could all do with an earlyish supper and a good night's sleep – especially you, Simon, after your ordeal last night.'

The others agreed, so Simon clambered up the heap of boulders and extinguished the hurricane lamp. Leaving most of the equipment in the cave, ready for the next day's work, they headed back towards the lake.

Earlier, they'd been so intent on getting to the cave that no one had given much attention to looking for wildlife. Now though, as they walked back through the trees, they took their time to look around them.

'Your best bet is to look up,' said Professor Gadling, doing so. 'The majority of a rainforest's wildlife lives up in the tree canopy.'

Everyone followed his example, gazing up between the immensely tall, straight tree trunks to the leafy world above, and they were rewarded with sightings of several  interesting animals – small monkeys, brightly coloured birds and, most exciting of all, a flying lizard that they glimpsed gliding between two treetops, its delicate body held airborne by rounded membrane wings.

'Ah, I was hoping we'd see some of them here,' said Professor Gadling. 'Your actual flying dragons, if a little smaller than those of legend. And they're just one of the many creatures in this part of the world that have evolved the ability to glide through the air. As well as the flying lizards and geckos, there are flying frogs, which can stretch the webbing of their large feet into four parachutes. Then there are flying snakes which can launch themselves from treetops by uncoiling themselves suddenly, and then glide by flattening their body and performing the same sort of sideways undulations that ordinary snakes do when moving along the ground. And there are gliding mammals such as the flying squirrel and a strange nocturnal creature called the colugo, both of which stretch membranes of skin between their four limbs.'

Had Zara not read about most of these creatures in books, she might have thought that they belonged in the category of Professor Gadling's not-quite-scientifically-proven species.

The flying lizard made another glide.

'Amazing,' said Gabrielle, studying the reptile's controlled flight with the appreciative eye of a fellow aviator. 'Dr Shariman wasn't exaggerating when he said this island was fascinating and beautiful.'

'It's a paradise,' agreed Marcia. 'If only the whole world could be like this – completely unspoilt by people.'

It occurred to Zara that if the whole world was empty of people, there'd be nobody around to know that it *was* a paradise. But she didn't want to start an argument, so said nothing.

Ben thought it was a bit of a shame that they weren't going to sleep here in the rainforest, like explorers he'd read about. He liked sleeping on board the flying boat, and he could see how that was far more practical for their expedition, but he was sure that spending the night slung between two trees in a hammock, surrounded by wildlife, would be an amazing experience.

They emerged from the forest back onto the lakeside. Now that they had a view of the sky once more, they could see that towering grey clouds were beginning to form overhead.

'Looks like there's going to be heavy rain before long,' said Professor Ampersand.

'Yes,' agreed Professor Gadling. 'Late afternoon downpours are a pretty typical weather pattern for tropical forests. They're not called rainforests for nothing.'

In less than an hour, Amy had ferried everyone back to the *Pelican Queen*. For now at least, the waters of the west-facing bay gleamed in the early evening sunshine, though the clouds building up over the island were spreading. The surface of the sea had a strange, almost oily smoothness, and the air felt even hotter and heavier than normal.

Once everyone had gathered in the *Pelican Queen*'s lounge, Wilfred took out the piece of jet carving from his biscuit tin and placed it next to the newly found piece. As everyone expected, the broken edges of each part fitted together perfectly to form a complete moth.

'It's a remarkable piece of craftsmanship,' said Professor Ampersand. 'Look how precisely that hole has been drilled sideways through the head, to make its two eyes. And look how intricate the pattern on the wings is.'

'I don't think the pattern can have been copied *exactly* from a real moth, though,' said Adam, looking at the jet sculpture carefully. 'On real moths, the wing markings are symmetrical, aren't they? But on this carved one, these squiggly lines on the right wings are quite a bit different from the ones on the left.'

'You're right,' agreed Professor Gadling. 'That seems to confirm that the pattern on this carving really is just a bit of artistic licence.'

'Yeah, must be,' said Simon.

'I suppose so,' said Sam, though without much conviction. For some reason he found himself dissatisfied with this explanation. The precisely etched lines of the pattern reminded him of something, but he couldn't think what.

'Well, we've had a brilliant first day here,' said Simon, standing up and heading through the aft doorway of the lounge. 'I think we've all earned a cold drink. How about I knock us up a jug of iced tea? I noticed that the fridge has an icebox, and we bought plenty of fresh lemons this morning, didn't we?'

'Sounds perfect, dear,' said Gabrielle. 'D'you want a hand?'

'No, I'm fine,' called Simon from the kitchen. 'I make a pretty mean iced tea, though I say it myself. You lot have a good sit down.'

'Hey, let's email Professor Hartleigh-Broadbeam and the others back home,' suggested Zara, going through to the short passageway that led off from the forward end of the lounge. 'We should tell them what we've found so far.'

'Go ahead, you lot,' said Professor Gadling to the children. 'And see if they've sent *us* any emails during the day. My laptop's on the office desk.'

The five children squeezed into the tiny cubby-hole office. Zara switched on Professor Gadling's laptop, opened up the email programme and first checked the inbox. There was a new message, with the subject name 'Pulau Gigi Naga Expedition'. But they could see from the sender's name that it wasn't from Professor Hartleigh-Broadbeam, Sharpe or Pottle, nor from Sam's parents. It was from Simon Arblinton.

'That's odd,' said Sam. 'How can Simon have sent us a message today, when he's been with us since yesterday?'

'It must be a message he sent before setting off from Thailand that got delayed somehow,' said Zara. 'Look, it's dated from five days ago, from just before we set off from the UK.' She clicked on the message's heading to open it, expecting it to say something like, 'Looking forward to seeing you in Malaysia on Tuesday.' But it didn't. The message that appeared said:

Hi Garrulous

Really sorry to hear the Pulau Gigi Naga expedition has had to be postponed at the last minute. Thanks for letting me know before I started setting off from the dig here in Thailand. Really hope you get the aircraft problem sorted soon. I can still get time off from this dig at short notice and rendezvous with you in Malaysia whenever you get there, so just let me know when you're finally setting off from the UK.

All the best,

Simon

Everyone read and reread the message, rather perplexed. 'That doesn't make any sense,' said Zara. 'What's all this about an aircraft problem and the expedition being postponed?'

'Look, the message that Simon's replying to is underneath,' said Ben. 'You can see from the heading that it was from Professor Gadling. Scroll down so we can read it.'

Zara did so, and everyone read this earlier message which, according to the time and date on its heading, had been sent to Simon just half an hour before he had replied.

Hello Simon

I'm terribly sorry, but due to an unforeseen major technical problem with one of our aircraft, we're going to have to postpone the expedition. Hopefully we may be able to fix it within the next few days, and set off then, but if not, we may need to put things off until early next year. You'd better stay put in Thailand for now, and I'll keep you informed of developments. Obviously we need to continue to keep the nature of the planned expedition a secret in the meantime.

Apologies for messing you around. I hope this doesn't disrupt your plans too much. Fingers crossed all will be back on track soon.

Best wishes,

Garrulous Gadling

'That makes even *less* sense,' said Marcia.

Simon appeared at the office doorway, carrying a tray with five glasses of iced tea on it. 'Emailing home?' he said. 'Good idea. I thought I'd bring your drinks through to you.'

'Thanks,' said Zara. 'Actually, we're trying to make sense of this old email of yours that's just arrived, and the email you were replying to.'

'What emails do you mean?' said Simon. Frowning, he studied the screen. Then his brow cleared. 'Oh, *that*,' he said. 'Gosh, has my email only just come through now? I sent it just after I got that email from Professor Gadling, five days ago, as you can see. Must've gone astray somewhere in cyberspace. My internet service provider is a bit unreliable, I'm afraid. Still, my reply didn't matter anyway, as it turned out. Just after I'd sent my reply, Professor Gadling emailed me again, letting me know that the whole aircraft problem had been sorted and that we were back on our original schedule after all.'

'But I don't remember any problem with either aircraft being discussed on the day before we set off,' said Marcia, 'or any talk about postponing the expedition.'

'Well, like I say, the problem turned out to be a total false alarm,' said Simon, 'and it was all resolved within no time.

So Professor Gadling probably didn't even bother mentioning it to you.' He proffered the tray towards them. 'Now, have a good drink before you get stuck into writing your email home,' he said. 'Take my word for it, it's easy to

 get dehydrated after you've been working all day in this tropical heat.'

They each took a glass. They were all thirsty, and the cold tea – served with lemon slices, sprigs of mint and masses of ice cubes – looked extremely refreshing.

But just before her glass reached her lips, Marcia felt a sudden pang of uneasiness in her gut. Something about the way Simon was encouraging them to drink the iced tea brought a memory flashing into her mind – an unpleasant memory of a time (shortly before she'd first met Zara, Ben, Sàm and Adam) when she'd been encouraged to drink various drinks with a similar slightly unnatural enthusiasm. And on that occasion, the drinks had been drugged.

This memory seemed to trigger all of Marcia's senses and, in that same split second, she was suddenly certain that Simon's explanation of the emails couldn't be true. Professor Gadling would never have taken it upon himself to tell Simon the expedition was postponed without even telling everyone else there was a problem. And as soon as she realised that Simon was lying, she could somehow suddenly see that his whole friendly manner was false. She also became suddenly aware that she could no longer hear any sounds of chatting from the adults in the lounge.

'Stop!' she warned the others. 'Don't drink!'

She bolted for the doorway. Simon's smile vanished, and he stepped sideways, trying to block her way. But Marcia was too quick for him. She barged past him and out into the passageway. At the entrance to the lounge she stopped, staring at the scene within, her terrible suspicion confirmed by what she saw.

Professor Gauntraker and Gabrielle lay lolled back in their seats, heads hung limply to one side. Professor Gadling and Wilfred were slumped forward over their tables. Professor Ampersand and Amy lay sprawled on the carpeted floor, their arms and legs at awkward angles. All six adults were totally motionless.

15

Six glasses lay near where the adults had slumped or fallen, spilling six puddles of cold tea, ice cubes, lemon slices and mint onto the tables and carpet.

Marcia felt a cold dread in her stomach. Had the adults been drugged . . . or poisoned?

She looked back to see Sam, Zara, Ben and Adam emerging from the office. For a couple of seconds, Simon tried to block their way, but then he seemed to give up the attempt and allowed them to pass him. They joined Marcia at the lounge doorway and gasped as they saw the stricken adults, unable to make sense of the scene.

'WHAT HAVE YOU *DONE* TO THEM?' Marcia yelled angrily at Simon, who was now standing behind them in the passageway, next to the office door.

'Everyone stay calm,' said Simon in a cold, unfamiliar voice. As he spoke, Marcia saw his right hand move to his trouser pocket – a pocket in which there was something bulky.

'Look, out!' she cried. 'He's going for a gun!'

Her words snapped the others out of their daze and into action. Zara was nearest to Simon and, with lightning speed, she made a grab for his wrist, hoping to stop him drawing the weapon. He stepped back, avoiding her grasp, but as he did so, Adam flung the contents of his glass at

Simon's feet. Simon slipped on the ice cubes and fell backwards, his head hitting the metal floor of the passageway with a crack. However, he was still conscious, and in a flash he finished pulling out the gun – a small, grey automatic.

But before Simon could take aim from his lying position, Ben launched a powerful kick at his hand, sending the gun flying from his grasp and into the cockpit, where it clattered under the pilot's seat. Ben charged onwards in a leaping stride over Simon. He had to get to the gun before Simon did. But Simon lunged after Ben, grabbing him by an ankle, yanking him back, and flinging him to the floor with violent force.

The others piled onto Simon, but he was too strong for them. Knocking them back with well-aimed punches and kicks, he scrambled to his feet, trampled over Ben, and dashed into the cockpit.

Zara watched Simon dive under the pilot's seat. They couldn't stop him getting the gun now, and it wouldn't take him long. 'RUN!' she shouted to the others, dragging Ben to his feet.

The five of them sprinted across the lounge, around and over the stricken bodies of Professor Ampersand and Amy, through the doorway at the other end and into the corridor. Sam slammed the lounge door behind them. It had no lock, but it would stop Simon from seeing where they were going, and Sam had a plan.

'QUICK!' he yelled loudly, as they ran past the kitchen and toilets. 'DOWN THE HATCH! WE CAN SHUT OURSELVES IN THE CARGO HOLD!'

But as he shouted these words, he shook his head furiously and shoved everyone away from the hatchway that led to the lower level, and towards one of the nearest bedroom cabins (Amy and Gabrielle's). The others cottoned on immediately, and slipped through the cabin doorway as quickly and as silently as they could.

Sam was last in. His instinct was to shut and latch the cabin door behind them. But realising that this would draw attention to their hiding place (and that the small brass latch would be no match for the gun's bullets), he pushed the door only to a half-closed position – the way it had been before they'd entered. He had only just done so when they heard the sound of Simon's feet running across the carpeted lounge floor, heard the door from the lounge being opened, and heard Simon racing along the corridor, getting nearer.

Everyone held their breath for fear that their panting would be heard. Sam was afraid that his thumping heart would be audible from the corridor. He stood poised by the ajar cabin door, ready to kick it shut and latch it if their deception failed, if it started to be pushed open . . .

But it didn't. To their relief, the children heard Simon climbing down the hatchway's metal ladder. They could hear him starting to shout as he descended to the lower level: 'GIVE YOURSELVES UP AND YOU WON'T BE HARMED. I'VE ONLY PUT THE OTHERS TO SLEEP. IT'S A COMPLETELY HARMLESS DRUG – WEARS OFF IN THIRTY-SIX HOURS.'

The children all felt a surge of relief that apparently the adults weren't dead, though the feeling was dampened somewhat by the thought that Simon might be lying. Whatever the case, they had no intention of obeying his instruction to give themselves up. Simon's voice had none of the friendly, laid-back warmth that it had had before, and the transformation was chilling. They were all stunned and shocked by the events of the last two minutes, unable to understand what was going on or what it all meant.

But there was no time to ponder that now. Sam had deliberately picked a cabin on the starboard side to hide in because he knew that the *Silver Turtle* was anchored just next to this side of the *Pelican Queen*. The little flying boat was the obvious means of escape, and the others nodded as Sam pointed to her through the cabin's porthole window. In fact, Marcia had already opened the porthole as fully as it would go, and was clambering through it.

She went through feet first and backwards, clinging to the porthole rim. She had to avoid making a splash. Ben held her wrists and lowered her down into the water, almost silently. Then he hurriedly went through himself, helped by Zara.

They were taking too long, fretted Zara. They could hear Simon crashing around in the hold, toppling crates and banging cupboard doors, but she knew he'd quickly run out of places to look down there. He was still shouting.

'COME OUT FROM WHEREVER YOU'RE HIDING! I DON'T WANT TO SHOOT YOU, BUT I WILL IF I HAVE TO. COME ON! TRUST ME. I MEAN YOU NO HARM. I ONLY WANT YOUR LITTLE PLANE. JUST DRINK THE TEA, AND WHEN YOU WAKE UP I'LL BE GONE – OUT OF YOUR WAY, FOR EVER.'

Zara made Adam and Sam go next, and went last herself. She dropped into the sea as quietly as she could and, like the others, swam breaststroke to avoid splashing. Even so, she expected at any second to hear gunshots and feel a bullet going into her back. Surely Simon must have realised he'd been tricked by now. He'd be racing back up the ladder, searching the cabins, looking through the portholes.

But the children reached the *Silver Turtle* unimpeded. They hauled themselves aboard, Ben and Marcia tumbling into the pilots' seats, Zara and Adam onto the seat behind, and Sam into the nose hatch, where he frantically started slicing the anchor line with his Swiss army knife. As soon as Ben saw that the line was cut, he flicked the starter switches on, revved the motors to full power, and took the little flying boat into a speeding take-off run across the water.

Now they had been heard and seen. Shots rang out from the *Pelican Queen. PTANG!* A bullet ricocheted off the *Silver Turtle*'s metal hull. Everyone instinctively kept low in their seats, but no bullets struck the plane's Plexiglas canopy. Ben pulled back his control column and the aircraft lifted away from the water.

They had taken off in the direction the plane had been facing – towards the shore – and Ben held this east-north-easterly course as they approached the beach.

'We should fly round the island a bit and land,' Zara shouted, above the noise of the air whistling past. 'Radio someone for help.'

'No,' Ben yelled back. 'Sounds like Simon knows how to fly, too. He'll come after us in the *Pelican Queen*, and if we land near here, he'll get us. We should make the most of our head-start – fly over the island and keep going over the sea until we reach one of the Spratly Islands. They're the nearest land. We can try and radio ahead for help as we go.'

'You're right,' agreed Zara. 'Go for it!'

The *Silver Turtle* sped over the strip of sand and up over the rainforest-covered slopes behind. To avoid the dangers of the cloud-covered craggy peaks, Ben steered a course that would take them across the southern end of the island, well to the right of the high central hills.

'Can you see what Simon's doing?' yelled Ben to Zara and Adam, who were looking back at the bay through the rear section of the canopy. 'Has he started the *Pelican Queen*'s engines, or is he still shooting at us?'

'Her propellers aren't turning,' reported Zara. 'I can't see Simon . . . No, wait – he's just climbing out onto the top of the cockpit. But we must be out of range of his pistol.'

'He's taking aim anyway,' added Adam, his sharp eyes able to roughly make out the distant figure's posture. Then a burst of orange flame flashed from the weapon being aimed at them – too big and bright for a pistol shot. And then he saw something streaking up towards them: something small and sleek that was emitting a thin trail of yellow flame and white smoke behind it.

'*A MISSILE!*' screamed Adam and Zara together.

The terror in their voices spurred Ben's already-heightened reflexes into immediate action. His hands wrenched the control column from side to side, while his feet pummelled the rudder pedals. The little plane banked, swerved and jinked erratically, changing course every couple of seconds.

But the tiny missile swerved too, responding to their every movement. And catching up fast. It was so close now that Zara could see every hi-tech detail of its streamlined khaki surface. She clasped Adam's hand. This was it. They were going to die.

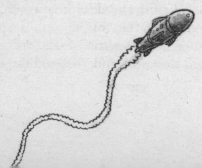

16

BLAM!

A deafening explosion. A blinding flash. A blast of smoke engulfing everything.

Zara found she was still conscious. And she could still feel Adam's hand in hers. Did that mean she wasn't dead? The smoke thinned, blown away by the rushing air. Now she could see Adam, shell-shocked but definitely alive; and Ben and Marcia, wrestling with the controls; and Sam, still in the nose hatch, just visible through the cracked and blackened windscreen. Where had the missile struck? There – the left motor. It was totally wrecked, its metal panelling burst and buckled, sparks and smoke streaming from its innards, propeller blades gone. Parts of the wing were badly damaged, too. Were they still flying? Only just. The stricken plane was starting to plummet into a nose dive.

'*BEN!*' screamed Zara. '*LEVEL OUT!*'

'*CAN'T!*' Ben shouted. '*CONTROL COLUMN'S NOT WORKING! USE YOURS, MARCIA!*'

'*IT'S JAMMED!*' yelled Marcia, already pulling desperately at the co-pilot's stick. Now sparks were bursting from the instrument panel. And the right motor was making a terrible noise. The angle of the dive became steeper and steeper, the treetops nearer and nearer.

Then, just when an almost vertical crash seemed

inevitable, Marcia felt her control column shift. Yanking it back, she brought the nose of the plane up. But they were still losing height. Not enough motor power. She couldn't stop them from hitting the trees.

CRRRUNCHH! The *Silver Turtle* crash-landed onto the tree canopy and for several seconds careered onwards through the upper foliage, her hull bucking and juddering violently as it smashed through hundreds of thin branches. Desperately gripping the sides of the nose hatch, Sam sank low in his seat as a blizzard of broken twigs and leaves sprayed over the aircraft. Then, BANG! – the left wing hit a thick tree trunk. The massive jolt nearly sent Sam flying from his seat, but he just managed to cling on as the little flying boat went into a chaotic diagonal fall down through the trees. Sam's view became a confused whirl of greenery. THUD. BANG. Their tumbling descent was punctuated by more horrendous jolts as the plane crashed from one big tree bough to another. CLUNK. SLAM. CRASH!

The last jolt *did* dislodge Sam from the nose hatch and

he felt himself falling helplessly through the air. Whump! He landed on his back. Couldn't breathe. Winded.

But after a few horrible moments, his lungs began to work again. Lying there, he checked that he could move all four limbs. All working. Nothing broken. The ground he was lying on was soft. Getting to his feet, he saw that he'd landed in a patch of mud and rotting vegetation. He'd been lucky. But what about the others? Several metres above him, what was left of the *Silver Turtle* was wedged nose down between the massive branches of a huge tree.

The forest was alive with the screeches and flappings of wildlife, panicked by the violent invasion of their world. But Sam could see no signs of life from the *Silver Turtle*. Feeling sick with dread, he got to his feet and yelled. 'Zara! Ben! Marcia! Adam!'

Marcia's head and shoulders emerged from the cockpit. She looked dazed and her forehead was bleeding. 'Sam!' she called down in a weak voice. 'Are you all right?'

'Yeah,' said Sam. 'Are you? And the others?'

'I'm OK,' said Marcia. 'Just cuts and bruises.'

'Same here, I think,' croaked Ben, getting up from under the instrument panel, rubbing his arm.

'And me,' said Zara. 'But Adam got flung out when we were crashing down through the trees.'

Sam turned to scan the forest floor, fearing the worst. 'ADAM!' he yelled.

'Here!' came Adam's voice. He was alive! Sam raced towards where the voice had come from, and found Adam caught up in a thorn bush. His clothes were torn and his skin was badly scratched and grazed, but otherwise he was in one piece. The bush, and the tree branches above, had broken his fall.

Sam helped Adam to extract himself from the tangle of

thorns and they made their way back to the others, who were climbing down to the ground, using the creepers that clung to the tree trunk.

Marcia looked up at the wrecked plane and let out a long breath. 'We're lucky to be alive,' she said.

'We wouldn't be if you hadn't pulled the plane out of that dive before we hit the trees,' said Ben. 'Well done.'

'Yeah, and well done for realising that Simon was trying to drug us,' added Zara.

'Well, he'd have got us if you and Ben and Adam hadn't disarmed him,' said Marcia, 'and if Sam hadn't tricked him into going down to the hold.'

Zara sat down on a fallen tree trunk. Since that terrible moment of finding the adults unconscious, she'd been running on adrenalin, concerned only with their immediate escape and survival. Now, the bewildering shock of everything that had just happened began to hit her fully, and she found she was shaking uncontrollably. Everything had changed so fast. Only a few minutes ago they'd been relaxing on the *Pelican Queen* after a happy and successful day, looking forward to supper. Now they were stranded in the middle of the rainforest, having narrowly escaping being killed by someone they had thought was their friend.

'I just don't understand,' she said. 'Simon seemed like such a nice guy. But he must've been planning to drug us all along. And he was prepared to *kill* us to stop us escaping. Where on earth did he get a missile-launcher from?'

'It must have been in his rucksack,' said Adam. 'He must have had it there all the time and must have run to get it when we took off.'

'I don't think he's really Simon Arblinton at all,' said Marcia. 'I think the real Simon Arblinton – the archaeologist Professor Gadling's friend recommended – is still in

Thailand. I reckon the man we've known as Simon must have hacked into the real Simon's email correspondence with Professor Gadling.'

'So he faked that email from Professor Gadling that we just saw, telling the real Simon that the expedition was postponed?' said Ben. 'So that he could take the real Simon's place by meeting us in Malaysia?'

'That's what I think,' said Marcia. 'And the email we just received on the laptop was the real Simon's reply to the fake message. I'm sure we weren't meant to get that. I'd guess that the fake Simon must have tampered with the real Simon's computer system so that any reply to the fake message got sent to him, instead of to us. But it looks like the real Simon's reply slipped through somehow and eventually got to us anyway, five days late. Anyway, that's my theory.'

'I think you must be right,' said Sam. 'The man we've known as Simon probably disguised himself to look and act like the real Simon, in case Professor Gadling's friend had given us a description.'

'I *thought* the glass in his glasses looked flat instead of curved like proper lenses,' said Adam. 'I noticed it when I picked them up for him last night. I should have said something, but it seemed a bit personal to ask him about his eyesight.'

'But why did he want to latch himself onto our expedition and drug us all?' asked Ben. 'If he just wanted to steal the *Silver Turtle*, like he claimed, there are much easier ways he could have done that.'

'Well, whoever he is and whatever his plan is,' said Zara, 'he's got control of the adults and of the only working plane. We're in the middle of the rainforest, the *Silver Turtle*'s radio's completely smashed, and it'll be dark in less than an hour. What are we going to do?'

A rumble of thunder rolled around the nearby hills. Looking up through the trees, the children could see that the clouds overhead were becoming a darker and darker grey. There was another burst of thunder, more violent than the first, and big drops of rain began to fall.

17

From his position on the top of the *Pelican Queen*'s cockpit canopy, the young man whom the children had known as Simon had watched the *Silver Turtle* crash into the tree canopy and disappear from view. The crash site was a couple of miles inland, and it took several seconds for the sounds of the plane hitting the trees to reach him, and then only faintly.

He swore. The children were almost certainly dead, and he'd wanted to avoid that. Not that he felt remorse. He'd had to stop them escaping, and it was their own fault that they'd forced him to use the missile-launcher. Little brats. They should have drunk the iced tea while they'd had the chance. No, the reason he had wanted to avoid killing his fellow expedition members was to avoid all the complications that such a crime would bring – a search for the missing people, a murder investigation if the bodies were found, a global police hunt for him when his body wasn't found with the others'.

Well, it was done now. The *Silver Turtle* – a major component of his plan – was out of the picture. But he wasn't going to let this setback ruin everything. He would carry on with his plan. He just needed to adapt it, that was all. He clambered back down into the cockpit and sat in the pilot's seat to think.

The central problem was how to get back to the cave quickly. He still had the *Pelican Queen*, but that was too big to land on the lake. Without the *Silver Turtle*, he was facing an arduous trek through the jungle, and that would take ages. There had to be another way . . . Yes! The solution came to him. He ran his modified plan through in his mind, and decided it would work.

Looking across to the island, he saw lightning flickering around the cloud-covered hills and heard the thunder. The whole sky was overcast now. Sheets of rain began to obliterate the entire island's outline and churn up the surface of the sea. Heavy rainfall wouldn't make his journey to the cave any easier, but he wasn't going to let it bother him. He was well equipped, he had a good plan, and he was going to succeed.

Marcia, Sam, Ben and Adam sat down with Zara on the fallen tree trunk as warm rain began to pour down.

'I think we should try to get back to the bay', said Ben, in answer to Zara's question asking what they were going to do, 'and see what Simon's up to – I mean the man who was pretending to be Simon. If he leaves the *Pelican Queen* to come ashore in the inflatable boat, we might get a chance to pinch the boat back. He probably thinks we're all dead or badly injured, so he won't be expecting us to come back. We could get out to the *Pelican Queen* and get away.'

'The *Pelican Queen*'s controls are a lot more complicated than the *Silver Turtle*'s,' Marcia pointed out. 'Do you think we could we manage a take-off?'

'Maybe not,' said Ben, 'but we could at least taxi her far out to sea – get ourselves and the adults safely away from the man, and leave him stranded. Then radio or email for help.'

'But he'd fire that missile-launcher at us again!' protested Zara, her voice shaky once more and full of fear. 'We were incredibly lucky not to be killed just now. It would be suicidal to give him a second opportunity to use it on us.'

'Look, we'd only risk trying anything if we were sure the man wasn't around or if he didn't have the missile-launcher with him,' said Ben. 'Maybe that's unlikely, but I think we should get ourselves to the edge of the forest behind the beach anyway, so that we're in the right place to take advantage of any safe chance that comes up. It's got to be a better bet than staying here and doing nothing.'

'You're right,' said Zara, making herself take several deep breaths. 'It's a good plan. Sorry for sounding panicky. It's just shock.'

Ben put an arm around his big sister. 'I'm just as shaken up as you are,' he admitted. 'The only reason I'm not a gibbering wreck is because you're here and because everyone's OK.'

'I'm pretty drained too,' said Marcia. 'We all need some food. Wasn't there half a packet of biscuits in the front of the *Silver Turtle*?'

Marcia and Adam, the most agile of the group, clambered up the big tree to the wrecked plane. It was a difficult climb, with the rain beating down on them and streaming down the tree trunk and creepers, but they managed it. As they climbed into the cockpit, they felt the hull shifting slightly in the branches, so they didn't hang about for long. In addition to the biscuits, they found an almost finished packet of boiled sweets. Had they been making a normal flight when they crashed, Amy's bag would have been on board, containing such useful items as a first aid kit and a map. But Amy had taken her bag onto the *Pelican Queen* after their day's flying. However, Adam remembered that Amy always kept a small torch in a pouch in the back of the pilot's seat, and found it there.

'Well done,' said Marcia. 'Could be useful later on.'

Back on the ground, they each shared out the biscuits and boiled sweets. There was nothing like enough of either to satisfy their hunger, but they all felt a bit better with the sugary food inside them.

'At least we've plenty to drink,' said Sam, catching rainwater in a large cupped leaf.

'Do you know which way we need to go, Ben?' asked Zara, trusting her brother's navigation skills.

'I think so,' said Ben, visualising their approximate position on a mental map of the island. 'I'm pretty sure that if we head roughly westward, we'll hit the coast somewhere near the beach.' From a trouser pocket, he took out his small compass, something he rarely went anywhere without. It had been a present from Professor Ampersand. The horrible image of his great-uncle and the others, slumped unconscious in the *Pelican Queen*'s lounge, came into Ben's head. They were only drugged, not dead, he told himself. They had to keep believing that the man had at least been telling the truth about that.

Ben took a westerly bearing, and the five children set off through the rainforest.

18

 On the *Pelican Queen*, the man worked quickly and efficiently. First, he went to his cabin and stowed the missile-launcher back into his rucksack. The missile-launcher was a brand-new ultra-compact model that could telescope down to the size of a hairdryer when not in use. It had cost him a lot of money, but, as had just been proved, it was a highly effective piece of kit.

The rucksack had been made to look rather ordinary and scruffy on the outside, but it, too, was actually an expensive and technically complex piece of equipment – fully waterproof and extremely secure, with concealed electronic locks on all the zips. He checked the rucksack's other contents: four more small heat-seeking guided missiles, identical to the one he'd just fired; a pair of night-vision goggles, which he'd be needing soon; and various other hi-tech items.

He went through to the lounge. The six adults were still fully unconscious, and he was confident that they would remain so for the next thirty-six hours, but he would take no chances. From one of the large side pockets of his rucksack he took out six pairs of handcuffs. They were lightweight and slender in design, but virtually indestructible and impossible to escape from. With them, he fastened each of the adults to the lounge's riveted-down chairs by both wrists. He would probably have to kill them soon anyway, he mused. Now that the children had been killed, it would be safer to leave no one alive. But he could make a decision about that later, when he had time to work out how to dispatch them without leaving any traces.

The two halves of the jet moon moth carving were still lying together on one of the tables. The man took a slim digital camera from the rucksack and took a close-up photograph of the ancient carving. Using the screen and controls on the back of the camera, he made some precise adjustments to enhance and highlight certain aspects of the image. Once he was satisfied, he switched the camera off and put it back into the rucksack.

Next, he dragged the inflatable boat and electric outboard motor aboard the *Pelican Queen*, and stowed them next to the aircraft's big loading door.

Finally, he went through to the office, where he dashed off a fake email from the children to Professors Sharpe, Pottle and Hartleigh-Broadbeam, and Sam's parents. Mimicking the sort of simple, upbeat writing style that Zara would have used, he reported that all was well, that they had arrived at Pulau Gigi Naga and had found the lake, but that they would attempt to find the cave tomorrow.

As he sent the email, it occurred to him that he could keep sending fake reassuring emails like this for the next week or two, to delay any search for the missing expedition until he was far away. And maybe his final fake email could say that they'd decided to fly on to somewhere else for some reason, so that the authorities' subsequent search for the missing planes and people would be centred on somewhere far from Pulau Gigi Naga. That way, the incriminating wreckage of the *Silver Turtle* and the bodies of the children might never be found.

Of course, the authorities would discover that the real Simon Arblinton had never joined the expedition, and then they would try to find out who he, the impostor, really was. But he was quite sure they'd draw a blank; he'd covered his tracks pretty well before joining the expedition. Even those fingerprints that the Malaysian police had taken from the knife handle wouldn't match those from any police records; he'd never been arrested anywhere in the world. No, although the authorities might suspect that their mystery man had something to do with the disappearance of the expedition, they wouldn't know who he was or whether he was still alive. In any case, he'd soon be so rich that he'd be beyond the reach of any police force, and able to afford a dozen new identities if necessary.

Time to get moving. He went forward to the *Pelican Queen*'s bows and raised the anchor.

The five children staggered on through the forest. Lightning and thunder continued to flash and crash overhead, and the rain had rapidly developed into a torrential downpour. Even though the tree canopy must have been blocking some of the rain, they had quickly been soaked to the skin. Although this wasn't making them cold – the rainwater was warm, and the atmosphere remained hot and steamy – the rain was having a bad effect on their progress. The already uneven ground had become extremely slippy underfoot, with rivulets of water sluicing downhill through the mud. The lower parts of the undulating forest floor became flooded, and at times the children had to clamber warily over natural bridges made by fallen trees. At other times, the only way to get though a flooded area was to wade waist-deep through channels of churning brown water, clinging to one another for support.

As well as water and mud, they encountered many areas of jungly vegetation which, without the parangs, were almost impossible to get through.

'I'm sure it's a good plan to get to the beach, Ben,' said Marcia, as they attempted to use sticks to beat a path through some thorny bushes, 'but what makes you so hopeful that the man will come ashore at all? From what he said, he was planning to steal the *Silver Turtle*. With that plane crashed, won't he just take the *Pelican Queen* instead and fly off in that?'

'I don't think stealing the *Silver Turtle* can have been his whole plan,' said Ben. 'Otherwise, like I said before, why go to all the bother of coming to the island with us? He didn't try to drug us until after Wilfred had shown us exactly where the cave was and after we'd confirmed that the skeleton was there.'

'You mean you think he's been planning to steal Wilfred's discovery?' said Sam.

'Yeah,' said Ben. 'I reckon his plan was to take the skull from Wilfred's tin, fly back up to the lake, take the skeleton from the cave, then fly away with it before we came round from the drug. Then he'd claim that it was his own discovery, and sell the skeleton to a museum for a fortune.'

'But he said he was planning to leave us all alive to go home,' pointed out Zara. 'If he'd done that, then the minute he'd publicly announced his "discovery", we'd have known where he was and have had him arrested. Even if he was really planning to kill us all along, the professors back home and Sam's parents would have worked out what he'd done the minute he went public with the skeleton.'

'Well, then maybe he's been planning to sell the skeleton secretly,' said Ben, modifying his theory, 'Perhaps there are private collectors who'd pay huge amounts for something as incredible as that. And he's got the jet moon moth, don't forget. That'd be worth a fortune, too. And maybe he's hoping there are more ancient artefacts buried waiting to be dug up in the cave.'

'But how did he know about the cave and the skeleton at all?' said Marcia. 'And how did he find out about our expedition?'

'He must have known the real Simon,' guessed Sam. 'Must have read his emails from Professor Gadling or something.'

'What about those men who attacked him in the car park at the turtle sanctuary?' said Zara. 'Do you think they were really just burglars, or do you think they've got something to do with all this?'

'That's a point,' said Sam. 'Maybe they're rival criminals who've also found out about the skeleton and wanted to stop the fake Simon getting here.'

'They certainly seem to be a pretty ruthless gang, attacking him with a knife like that,' said Marcia. 'Maybe the fake Simon's expecting them to follow him here to the island in a boat; it would explain why he's carrying something as lethal as a missile-launcher.'

'Well, whoever they are and whoever the fake Simon is,' said Zara, 'we seem to have got ourselves caught up with some really dangerous people.'

'We'll get away,' said Ben optimistically. 'You can see why I'm hopeful that the fake Simon might leave the *Pelican Queen* and the adults unattended for long enough for us to get away. Without the *Silver Turtle*, he'll have to trek miles uphill through the rainforest to get back to the cave. He'll be gone for ages.'

Just then, the five children heard a distant sound cutting through the noise of the falling rain. It was a rumbling sound, and at first Zara thought it was just more thunder. But it quickly became obvious that it wasn't. It was the familiar growl of three large aero-engines starting up.

'The *Pelican Queen*!' exclaimed Sam.

'He's leaving,' said Marcia. 'He must have decided not to bother getting the skeleton now, and to get away with just the skull and the moon moth carving while he has the chance.'

'It doesn't leave my plan looking good,' said Ben. And it didn't leave the position of the adults looking good either, though no one wanted to say it.

'Maybe he's just taxiing nearer to the beach,' suggested Adam hopefully.

But the pitch of the engines was already rising to that of a full-speed take-off run. And after that, the engine noise grew steadily more distant, until it became inaudible.

'He's gone,' said Ben. He couldn't think what they were going to do now. The *Pelican Queen* was gone, taking away the six adults, and taking away their only means of contacting the outside world for help.

19

'We should keep heading for the beach anyway,' said Zara decisively. She knew that they mustn't give in to despair. They had to stay focused on a plan of action. 'We'll have more chance of getting help if we get ourselves to the shore.'

'Yeah,' said Sam. 'We might be able to signal a passing ship tomorrow.'

Everyone knew that they hadn't seen any ships going past since arriving at the island, but no one said so.

They struggled on through the forest, finding a route between the trees that kept them more or less on the westerly compass bearing. But the ceaseless torrential rain was making the ground ever more muddy and slippy, and in the darkening gloom, it was becoming impossible to see where was safe to tread. Everyone had a few falls, adding more bruises to their already sore and battered limbs. They were also all starving hungry. Progress became slower and slower.

'Look, let's face it: we're not going to reach the beach tonight,' said Marcia at last. 'It'll soon be properly dark, and someone will break a leg if we try to keep going when it's pitch-black.'

'You're right,' said Zara. 'We'll have to wait until dawn before going any further. But sleeping on the ground with all this mud and water's going to be impossible.'

'Yeah, we should try to make some sort of raised sleeping platform,' said Ben. 'It's not just to get out of the mud and water; it stops you getting eaten alive by all the insects that live on the ground. I saw them making one on a TV programme about jungle survival. Mind, it wasn't bucketing down with rain on TV, and they started making it about two hours before it got dark. I reckon *we've* got about fifteen minutes.'

'Let's start then,' said Zara. 'What do we need to make it?

'On TV, they used bamboo poles lashed together with creepers and vines,' said Ben. 'There are plenty of creepers around here. I haven't see any bamboo, but we can use other wood, obviously. The difficult part's going to be cutting ourselves the bits of wood we need without a parang. The upright support stilts will have to be quite thick to be strong enough.'

'We might not need to cut anything for the upright supports,' said Marcia. 'Couldn't we build the platform between those trees over there, so that their trunks are the upright bits?' She was pointing to a group of slender, relatively short trees which looked young and were growing close together.

'Good thinking,' said Ben, as they all hurried over to inspect them. 'If we could lash a good framework of long sticks between these four trees, about a metre off the ground, I think that'd work.'

'And we could bend the tops of the trees over and work the branches into a kind of roof frame,' suggested Sam. 'Then we could cover the whole thing with extra leaves from other trees and bushes.'

'Yeah, and we should cover the sleeping platform with leaves and bits of springy bushes,' said Ben, remembering what he'd seen them do on television.

They worked quickly. Sam, Zara and Ben gathered together a supply of long sticks and branches, either finding them on the ground (though many of these were too rotten and weak for the job), snapping them off trees, or hacking them off with the saw blade on Sam's Swiss army knife. Meanwhile, Marcia and Adam ripped several metres of strong creeper from some of the bigger trees nearby.

Then Zara went and hacked off armfuls of foliage from

various bushes, while Marcia and Sam worked on creating the roof frame, and Ben and Adam worked on the platform. They started the platform by lashing their four strongest long sticks between the four trees, to form an approximate rectangle of about two metres squared. Then they laid the other sticks at all angles across the frame and tied them in place, building up a rough mesh.

Once they'd tested the platform, to make sure it supported their weight, they all piled up the bushiest greenery that Zara had collected onto the makeshift platform, and used the flattest, broadest leaves to cover the roof. By this time, the brief twilight had faded to inky darkness, and they finished the job by torchlight, using Sam's keyring torch as well as the one they'd retrieved from the *Silver Turtle*.

'It's pretty good,' said Zara, and indeed it was. It was not the well-organised expedition camp of Ben's dreams, with mosquito-netted rainproof hammocks and a campfire. Nor was the structure as well worked out as Sam would have liked, if he'd had an afternoon to spend designing it in his notebook. The platform looked more like a nest than a bed, and the roof was only keeping out half the rainwater that fell on it. But for a rush job built in an emergency, it was a remarkably good piece of work.

Exhausted, sore, and drenched with sweat, rainwater and mud, the five children clambered onto the platform.

'We'd better switch off our torches and save the batteries,' said Sam.

'Yeah,' said Zara, 'but just give the platform a quick scan first, to check we're not about to lie down on any snakes or big spiders or anything that I might have collected with these bits of bush without noticing.'

Sam helped Zara do so willingly. Although he didn't like to admit it, he wasn't keen on spiders and big insects. However, they saw nothing living on the wet foliage except a few tiny bugs and flies.

'Looks clear enough,' said Sam. 'Let's hope none crawl onto the platform during the— *Urgh!* What's that on my arm?'

'It's a leech!,' said Marcia, looking at the small, slimy fattening thing that was latched onto Sam's bare arm. 'AAH! I've got one too, on my ankle.'

It turned out they were all being dined on by several leeches (though fortunately none had swollen to the size an aubergine in the way described by Professor Gauntraker). They pulled off the ones they could spot – a tricky job, as the leeches made every effort to stretch their heads forward and reattach themselves while being removed – and flung them as far away as they could.

'You'd have thought we'd have noticed bites like these sooner,' said Sam, examining his bleeding wound.

'They use a special chemical when they bite you which

stops you feeling it,' said Zara, who had been reading about leeches before the expedition. 'And they put another chemical in your blood to stop it clotting while they're drinking it. That's why our bites are bleeding so much. But they'll stop bleeding in a minute,' she added, noticing how queasy Sam was looking. 'Well, we'd better get some sleep.'

They switched off the torches and everyone lay down.

20

Adam, lying between Marcia and Zara, and certain that his four older friends would somehow get them all out of this situation safely, was asleep within ten minutes.

The others couldn't get to sleep for ages. There seemed to be too few leaves to make an effective mattress, and they could feel every sharp and bumpy bit of the sticks beneath. And, on the restricted space of the creaky platform, it was impossible to roll over in an attempt to find a more comfortable position without disturbing everyone else.

After a while, the rain stopped, but although this brought about a decrease in the amount of water dripping down on them, it also triggered an increase in the volume of insect and animal sounds. The children had thought the insect noises loud the night before, when they had been sitting on Dr Shariman's veranda. But now, with so many thousands of insects surrounding them at such close proximity, the noise seemed ten times greater – a relentless, high-pitched throbbing of cicadas accompanied by a background frenzy of buzzes, clicks and chirrups from other species. And from time to time, the children heard the maddening whine of mosquitoes close to their ears. It was impossible to see or slap the mosquitoes in the pitch darkness, and impossible, they knew, to prevent them from feeding on their blood.

There were other animal noises, too – unearthly, resonant

booming calls, repeated over and over again, that seemed to be coming from somewhere above them; sporadic shrieks and squeals of unknown life-and-death struggles being fought in the undergrowth around them; and all sorts of rustles, snuffles and grunts, some of which seemed to be coming from the ground directly beneath the sleeping platform. The children could only imagine what kind of creatures might be making all of these sounds, and what kind of creatures might be about to invade their sleeping platform.

As Marcia lay awake, she remembered how, only that afternoon, she'd said that this island was a paradise because it consisted of nothing but nature, unspoilt by people. She admitted to herself now that if a modern man-made building with snake-proof walls, mosquito-netted windows, air-conditioned rooms and proper comfortable beds were miraculously to materialise around them, then far from spoiling this rainforest, it would vastly improve it. And the only thing that was making this close encounter with nature bearable at all, the only thing keeping her from breaking down in terror, was the fact that other people were here with her.

Zara was certain that she wouldn't get to sleep at all. She couldn't believe that *anyone* ever managed to sleep in a rainforest. In addition to being impossibly noisy, the atmosphere seemed as stiflingly hot as it had been during the day. She lay there in the blackness, feeling uncomfortable, scared and, above all, sick with worry. She was worried about the adults, worried about being stranded on the island, worried about poisonous snakes and spiders, and worried about their many scratches, cuts and leech bites turning septic – a real danger, she knew, in this humid climate.

Ben found that the terrifying moments just before their plane crash kept replaying in his head – the terrifying moment when the *Silver Turtle* had been plummeting into a dive; the horrible feeling of finding his control column dead; the awful feeling of not being able to do anything to prevent their seemingly certain death.

Eventually though, in spite of the noise, and in spite of their worries and fears, Marcia, Zara and Ben drifted off to sleep. Sam was the last to be left lying awake. Normally his practical, optimistic nature prevented him from dwelling on worries too much, but his nervousness of giant spiders and insects was making him jittery. Whenever he thought he was dropping off, a rustle in the leaves around him would startle him back to full consciousness.

A couple of hours after the rain had stopped, Sam became aware that the sky overhead had cleared of cloud. Looking up through the many gaps in their makeshift roof, and through the spaces in the tree canopy high above, he could see stars. And after a while, the full moon (which he knew must have risen just after sunset) came into view overhead. Shafts of moonlight beamed down through the trees, dimly illuminating the mist and parts of the under-growth.

In the pale blue light, Sam saw a large dark shape flapping slowly and silently past the head end of the sleeping platform. It was a huge moth, bigger than Sam's hand. Its front wings were angular, and its back wings ended in long, trailing tendrils – a moon moth. And a moon moth that, in the moonlight at least, appeared to be totally black.

Sam's curiosity overrode his insect phobia and he switched on his torch, catching the moth in a tight circle of bright light. It switched course and started heading towards the torch, as did about a dozen other flying insects, and

Sam quickly turned the torch off again. But his brief illuminated glimpse had been enough to confirm that the moon moth was indeed velvety black all over.

Sam watched the moth steer back onto its original flight path and fly to a bush that was covered in large, pale flowers. It visited each bloom in turn – collecting pollen with its tongue, Sam guessed – then flapped gracefully away, merging into the darker shadows of the forest until it had vanished.

Sam shut his eyes and found that, somehow, picturing the moth going serenely about its business had a calming effect on his brain, and kept his scarier mental images of other giant insects at bay. He now found that he could ignore the nearby rustlings of unseen creepy-crawlies, and within a few minutes he finally slipped into sleep.

21

Marcia was woken by a loud, high-pitched whooping sound. As she opened her eyes, she discovered that dawn was breaking. The forest was enveloped in clouds of steamy mist that were rising slowly from the ground. The mist was grey in the shadows, but glowed amber where the rays of the morning sunlight caught it.

The whooping noises, which were clearly being made by several individual animals, were coming from the tree-tops somewhere nearby, and echoing around the forest. They had woken the others, too.

'I think it's gibbons singing,' said Zara. 'I read about them in a book. They do it at dawn.'

Singing was a good description; it was quite a musical sound, with notes that rose in pitch, volume and speed towards the end of each cadence. Marcia found the sound beautiful, rather than unnerving like the strange animal calls of the night before. Maybe it was because she knew what was making this sound, or maybe it was because it was dawn. Whatever the reason, as she lay there listening to the gibbons' song and watching the shapes of the for-est emerge from the golden mist, Marcia found her appre-ciation of nature returning. The buzzing, chirruping, living forest now seemed awe-inspiring rather than terri-fying. This place *was* a paradise, even if it was a scary and dangerous sort of paradise in the middle of the night.

'Look,' whispered Adam, pointing upwards through one of the open ends of their shelter. Through the mist, the dark shapes of a pair of gibbons could be seen swinging and tumbling playfully around the treetops with incredible agility. The children watched them for half a minute, before the small apes swung away out of sight again, back in the direction the singing was coming from.

'Well, we'd better get moving,' said Zara, swinging her legs down from the sleeping platform. 'The sooner we get to the beach, the sooner we've a chance of being rescued and getting help.'

Beautiful though daybreak in the rainforest was, it did nothing to lessen their desperate worry about what had happened to the adults. Where was the *Pelican Queen* now? wondered Zara. The big flying boat could have flown hundreds of miles away during the night. She clung to a tiny hope that the man who'd pretended to be Simon might have left the adults unharmed on the beach before flying away, but she knew that this wasn't very likely.

'Just let me get rid of these leeches,' said Ben, 'and then we'll be off.'

Everyone had acquired a few new leeches during the night, on their arms, ankles and necks. As they sat on the edge of the platform removing them, Sam told them about the black moon moth he'd seen in the night.

'So there must be a black subspecies native to this island,' said Zara. 'The carving was made out of jet for good reason

– to make it realistic.'

'Did it settle around here?' asked Ben, hoping that he might still be able to see it.

'No,' said Sam. 'It hung around that bush over there with the white flowers for a while, but then it—'

He stopped mid-sentence. In the undergrowth, some way beyond the bush he'd been pointing at, his eyes suddenly spotted a khaki sunhat. Someone was crouching behind a patch of dense, jungly greenery, watching them.

As soon as Sam stopped talking, the watcher seemed to sense that they'd been spotted, and turned and ran. Though mist and leaves obscured his view, Sam caught a glimpse of the fleeing figure and saw that it was a child – probably aged about four, judging from the height, and probably a girl, judging from the length of the  fair hair. He couldn't see her face, only the back of her. She was wearing a short-sleeved green shirt, and her arms looked tanned. That was all Sam was able to take in before she disappeared from sight.

'Hey! Wait!' Sam cried, leaping from the sleeping platform and racing off in pursuit. He reached the place where the child had been, and charged on through the undergrowth, ignoring the scratches of thorns, following the sounds of rustling foliage ahead. 'Wait!' he shouted again. He was following what seemed to be some sort of narrow animal track that twisted and turned through the dense bushes, so he was pretty sure he was going the same way as the girl.

After a while the bushes petered out, and he found that the path had led him into a small gully with high, moss-covered rocks on either side. Sam kept running and found that the gully quickly narrowed, until the two rock-faces joined together in a dead end. No sign of the girl.

'Where are you?' he yelled, checking behind the few boulders that lay on the gully floor. 'Come back! We need your help!' But there was no answer.

The gully had a strange atmosphere, stiller and quieter than the rest of the forest, and even more shadowy. The mist here hung motionless in the warm air. And the canopy formed by the trees growing along the tops of both rock-faces seemed especially dense, giving the deep shade below a particularly greenish quality.

The lonely gloom of the place was beginning to make Sam feel a bit spooked, and he was glad when Ben, Zara, Marcia and Adam appeared at the open end of the gully, running to join him.

'Who were you chasing, Sam?' asked Ben, panting as they reached him. 'Who were you yelling at?'

'If you saw someone, we should be careful,' said Zara. 'It could be one of the men who attacked Simon. I mean the fake Simon. They might have followed him here.'

Sam shook his head. 'It wasn't one of them,' he said. 'It was just a young child.' He quickly told them everything about the figure that he'd managed to glimpse.

'Hmm,' said Zara. 'I agree that it doesn't seem likely that a violent gang who were here to steal the skeleton would have brought a young child with them. But then, who *is* this girl you saw, and what is she doing here? This island is uninhabited.'

'There must be other people visiting the island we don't know about,' said Sam. 'A group of naturalists, or a family travelling in a yacht or something who've stopped off here. That's why I ran after the girl. There must be adults with her who could help us.'

'I wonder why she ran away,' said Ben.

'Shyness, I suppose,' said Sam. 'She got startled when she realised I'd seen her peeking at us. And maybe she doesn't speak English, so she didn't know what I was saying. Anyway, there's no sign of her here. She must have swerved off into the bushes, somewhere before the track reached this gully.'

'She'll have gone back to the adults she's with to tell them about us,' said Marcia, 'and they're bound to come and check us out. We should go back to our sleeping platform so they can find us.'

'Hang on,' said Adam, who had been examining the gully floor. 'There are footprints here.'

They all joined him and saw that he was right. In a patch of soft mud near the base of the left-hand rock-face were two footprints that looked as if they'd been made by a pair of boots. The sole pattern was not unlike that of their own jungle boots, but the shoe-size was much smaller than any of theirs.

'So she *did* come this way,' said Zara.

'The right footprint is more than a metre in front of the left one,' Adam pointed out, 'so I think she was still running. And the footprints point towards this bit of rock-face.'

'So she must have jumped at the rock-face and clambered up it,' said Ben.

'But I'd have seen her climbing!' insisted Sam. 'She *couldn't* have made it to the top before I got here. Look how steep and slippy that bit of rock-face is – how steep and slippy *all* the rock-faces are. A child as young as her couldn't have scaled any of them that quickly. I don't think *anyone* could. I must only have been a few hundred metres behind her.'

Zara paced back to the other side of the gully floor to get a better view of the rock-face the footprints pointed to. 'Maybe she didn't climb all the way to the top,' she said. 'There's a ledge halfway up. I can't see onto it, but it could be wide enough for someone to hide on.'

Marcia stepped back to join Zara and called up to the ledge, which was about seven metres above them. 'Are you up there?' she asked, trying to sound as friendly and gentle as possible. 'If you're up there, please let us know. You don't have to worry; we won't harm you. Are your parents nearby?'

There was no reply.

'I'd better go up and check it,' said Marcia.

'Yeah,' agreed Sam. 'Though I honestly don't think she could even have got *that* high in the time she had.'

It took three minutes for Marcia to reach the ledge. This slow climbing time certainly seemed to lend weight to Sam's argument, although Marcia was climbing with particular caution. A fall and a twisted ankle here would be no joke.

'Is she there?' called Zara.

'No,' Marcia, called down, 'there's no one. But I think she might have come this way. Come up and see.'

Puzzled, the others climbed the rock-face until they could see what Marcia had brought them up to look at. At the back of the ledge was the entrance to a cave.

22

The dark hole was even smaller than the entrance to the cave near the lake. It was about a metre wide and only half a metre high in the middle, which is why it hadn't been visible from the ground, even though the ledge was fairly narrow. The hole was also partially concealed by a row of ferns trailing down from above, which meant it wouldn't have been easy to spot, even from the top of the opposite rock-face.

'Even if she could have managed the climb quickly enough, do you really think she would have gone into there?' said Sam doubtfully. 'If she's so timid that she ran away from us, it's hard to believe she'd be brave enough to go into a hole as small and dark as that.'

'There are bits of mud round here, though,' said Adam, pointing to the back of the ledge. 'They could have got scraped off her boots.'

Zara clambered fully onto the ledge, lay on her stomach and put her head into the hole. The cave's interior seemed to be a sort of rugged tunnel, not much wider than the entrance, that sloped diagonally downwards through the rock, fading into total blackness after a few metres. 'Hello!'

Zara called. 'Are you in there? You don't need to hide from us.' From the resonance of her voice, Zara could tell that the cave tunnel went on for a long way. She turned back to the others. 'I can't hear anyone moving about down there,' she reported.

'Wait!' said Ben, who had joined his sister at the cave mouth. 'I think I can just hear *something*.'

Everyone else squeezed onto the ledge, and they all leaned forward and listened. From somewhere deep down in the cave came the very, very faint sound of breathy whimpering, the sound of someone crying while trying to remain silent.

Sam and Zara took the two torches from their pockets and shone them into the cave. Now they could see that the course of the cave tunnel twisted and turned as it disappeared downwards. They could see no sign of the girl, though. The whimpering was coming from the blackness beyond the range of the torch beam.

'We've got to go down there and help her,' said Sam, crawling through the entrance and turning round so he could clamber down the tunnel feet first. 'She's scared and she might have hurt herself. It's my fault. If I hadn't chased her, she wouldn't have tried to hide in here. Come on.'

'All right,' said Zara, following Sam in, 'but be careful. Don't squeeze through any gaps that you can't get back out of.' She knew Sam was right – they had to help the girl – but she felt very uneasy, confined in the narrow tunnel. She looked up at Marcia, Ben and Adam, who were waiting to descend behind her. 'Maybe you three should wait out there until we check that it's safe,' she suggested.

'OK,' said Marcia. 'Don't go too far.'

Sam and Zara followed the turns of the tunnel's downward-sloping course, using their hands and feet to stop themselves slithering too fast. For a while they could look back up the way they had come to see the cave entrance – a shrinking but comforting beacon of daylight. But after scrambling round a particularly sharp corner, the entrance disappeared from view, and their only sources of light were the torches.

As expected, the breathy crying grew louder as they went further down into the cave. Presumably the girl could hear them coming, and the sobs kept stopping for a few seconds, as if she was trying extra hard to remain silent by holding her breath. Sam and Zara kept calling to her, making their voices as reassuring as possible, but still they could get no answer.

It was hard to judge how far down from the cave entrance the sloping tunnel was taking them, but after descending for two or three minutes, Sam was pretty sure they must now be below the level of the gully floor. He was beginning to wonder if the narrow tunnel would go on for ever when he emerged into a spacious natural chamber.

Zara joined him. The whimpering had stopped just before they'd entered the chamber, and for a moment they stood still without speaking, straining for any sound of it resuming. But they could hear nothing. They shone their torches around, illuminating the chamber's curved rock walls and the stalactites hanging from its high ceiling, as they tried to see which way the girl might have gone.

'There!' said Zara. In her torch beam they could see a roughly arched opening to another cave tunnel, leading out from the opposite end of the chamber.

'That must be where she's gone,' said Zara, as they made their way towards the tunnel, negotiating the stony forest of stalagmites that covered the chamber's floor.

As they drew closer, Sam spotted something else. 'Look!' he exclaimed.

'Wow!' said Zara.

The rock around the tunnel entrance had been elabo-rately carved. The two sides of the natural archway had been sculpted into a pair of trees, with a variety of carved animals inhabiting the branches. Zara could identify monkeys, parrots, tree-frogs and lizards, and was sure there were other creatures to be spotted among the carved stone leaves. And over the archway, a hornbill had been rendered in mid-flight between the two treetops. The level of detail was remarkable, as was the realism of the animals' poses.

'If this was carved by the extinct human species, they must have used this cave as well as Wilfred's,' said Zara. 'These carvings must be really, really old. We're probably the first people to look at them for thousands of years!'

'Except for the girl we're following,' Sam pointed out. Something occurred to him. 'The girl must have already known about this cave to have run straight for it when I chased her. Maybe her parents are cavers, or archaeologists, who've been exploring this cave system.'

'Maybe,' said Zara. 'Or maybe she's just been using this cave as a pretend hideout to play in.'

They paused at the new tunnel's entrance and shone their torches down it. After ten metres or so, the tunnel curved away to the left and out of sight. Still they couldn't hear the girl's crying or any footsteps.

'Come on,' said Zara, and they entered the tunnel, calling out for the girl as they went. This tunnel was considerably easier to move along than the one they had just scrambled down. It was tall enough to walk upright, and barely sloped downwards at all.

Once they rounded the first corner, all they could see was another bend, some distance ahead. Still no sign of the girl.

'She must have a torch to have got this far,' said Zara. 'You'd think we'd be able to see at least a glimmer of light from it.'

'She must have got really far ahead,' said Sam. 'This tunnel could go on for miles. But we'd better keep going until we find her. She could get really lost down here.'

'So could we,' said Zara. 'I think we should nip back and get the others before we go any further. We should stick together. And they'll be wondering if we're all right.'

They retraced their steps back to the cave chamber.

'Maybe I should wait here while you go up and get the others,' said Sam, 'in case the girl decides to come back and find us. If no one's here, she might disappear deeper into the caves again instead of coming out.'

'That makes sense,' said Zara. 'But are you sure you'll be all right down here by yourself?'

Contemplating this, Sam felt less sure about his suggestion. It was pretty spooky in the cave chamber, even with Zara here with him. But he told himself to be rational. It was perfectly safe here. 'I'll be fine,' he said. 'As long as you're back quickly.'

'I'll be no time,' promised Zara. 'I'll just clamber back up until I can see daylight, then call for the others to come down.'

Sam watched Zara disappear back up the first tunnel. With only his own small torch now illuminating the chamber, the rock formations looked even more shadowy and the carvings even more mysterious. In the silent, still atmosphere, Sam found himself wondering what it would be like to be trapped down here, or lost, then quickly tried to push this horrible thought out of his mind.

He peered into the gloom of the second tunnel, wondering how far it went. Was the girl half a mile along it by now? Or was she hiding just past the point they'd got to, about to overcome her shyness and come back?

Suddenly a single, stifled sob resonated through the chamber, making Sam jump. And it hadn't come from the tunnel. It had come from nearer than that – from somewhere inside the chamber.

Sam turned and shone the torch all around the chamber. No one. Then he spotted something in the floor: a dark crevice, obscured by the stalagmites and their shadows. Sam made his way to the edge and shone his torch down.

At the bottom of the crevice, about four metres below him, was the girl. She sat in the circle of torchlight, hunched over with her head down, still covered by her khaki sunhat. The hat shook slightly, and her shoulders trembled. She was sitting in an awkward position and had both hands inside the top of her left jungle boot, rubbing her ankle. Sam guessed that she'd twisted it falling down the crevice. He and Zara might easily have fallen down it themselves if they'd come across the chamber a slightly different way.

'It's OK,' said Sam, starting to clamber carefully down the crevice to her. He hoped his voice sounded reassuring, even if she didn't understand English. 'We can get you out of there no problem and take you back to your parents.' Still the girl wouldn't reply, or even look up at him. 'The others will be here in a minute,' he added as he neared the bottom. 'We'll all help you.' He glanced upwards, looking to see if Zara's torchlight was returning to the chamber above them. Not yet.

Whap! Without lifting her head, the girl struck out with her right hand, knocking the torch from Sam's grasp. It went clattering across the bottom of the crevice and went out.

Pitch blackness. Total pitch blackness. Sam cried out in panic. He felt and heard the girl scrambling past him, heading upwards out of the crevice. He grabbed out at her, blindly and instinctively. His fingers grasped something that felt like some kind of a cord, and for a second it seemed to hold the girl back. Then he felt the cord go loose in his hand and he knew it had snapped. He was vaguely aware of hearing something small clattering down beside him. Then he heard scrabbling sounds above, and knew that the girl had got out of the crevice and was escaping across the chamber. If she did have a torch, she wasn't switching it on, since everything remained inky black.

Left alone in the utter darkness, Sam's panic and claustrophobia increased. He shouted out for help as he frantically groped around for his torch. Couldn't find it. Couldn't feel anything but rock. He started to try to climb up the crevice sides but slipped, banging his shin.

The knock forced him to calm himself down. His shin was OK, but he realised he could seriously injure himself trying to climb out when he couldn't see. He should stay still and wait. Wait for Zara to come back with the others.

The three minutes he waited felt like an age, during which all he could hear was his own fast, shaky breathing and racing heart. Then, at last, he heard the others' voices, and saw the beam of their torch flickering across the space above the crevice.

'Sam?' called Zara's voice.

'Down here,' he yelled back. 'There's a crevice. Don't fall into it.'

His four friends appeared at the top of the crevice, looking down at him. They helped him climb out, and he told them what had happened.

Marcia, Ben and Adam were shown the tunnel leading out of the chamber, and the carvings around its entrance. They were as amazed and impressed by these as Zara and Sam had been, though it was the mystery of the girl that seemed the most pressing matter.

'So the girl didn't speak to you?' asked Marcia.

'Wouldn't even look up at me,' said Sam. 'She just huddled herself into a ball.'

'Why is she so scared of us?' wondered Ben.

A possible theory occurred to Zara. 'Maybe her parents – or whatever adults she's here with – don't have permission to be here on the island,' she said. 'We certainly weren't told there was anyone else exploring here. Maybe Sam's right, that they're archaeologists who've been exploring these caves, and already know more about the people who lived here than we do and want to keep their discoveries secret. So maybe the girl was told not to go near anyone from our expedition or let anyone see her, in case they got into trouble.'

'I suppose that could be it,' said Marcia. 'Well, even if her parents aren't meant to be here, they'd surely help us in an emergency like ours, wouldn't they? Like you said before, if they've brought a young child here with them, they're not likely to be part of some dangerous gang. If we can find the girl, we'll probably be able to find people with a radio or email or something.'

'I hope so,' said Zara. Throughout all the morning's events, her anxiety about her great-uncle and the other adults on the *Pelican Queen* had remained uppermost in her mind. 'We have to find the girl anyway, before she gets lost.'

'She must really have run along this tunnel this time,' said Sam.

'Yeah,' said Ben. 'She certainly didn't come back up our tunnel when we were coming down. We'd better get going and try to catch her up.'

'Hang on,' said Sam, rushing back to the crevice. 'Let me try to find my torch first. And I've remembered something. I grabbed some sort of cord she was wearing as she escaped. It snapped and something fell to the ground. I don't know what it was, but if we can find it, it might give us some sort of clue about her.'

With Amy's torch, they were able to find Sam's keyring torch lying at the bottom of the crevice. The battery cover had been knocked off, which is why it had gone out. Fortunately, the cover and the two little batteries were found nearby, and Sam was able to get the torch working once more.

Even with both torch beams, finding the broken cord and whatever had been attached to it proved harder. But eventually, Adam spotted the cord – a length of dark, shoelace-thin twine – lying at the bottom of the crevice. Marcia knelt down to get it, and then searched the area closely.

'Here,' she said, retrieving something else from a cranny in the crevice's floor. She held it up for them all to see.

Everyone stared, stunned with surprise. The object was a black jet carving of a moon moth.

'It looks identical to ours,' said Ben. 'Except it's still in one piece.'

'It's not quite identical, though,' said Adam. 'The pattern of lines carved into its wings is different from the pattern on ours. Similar, but not the same.'

'The girl must have found it,' said Zara. 'Either in this cave, or somewhere else on the island. You think she had it hanging on the cord, Sam?'

'Yeah,' said Sam. 'I couldn't see it when I was looking down at her, because her hat was blocking my view, but I reckon she must have been wearing it round her neck like a pendant. I think the cord must have been threaded through the moth's eyeholes until it snapped when I grabbed it. See, the hole's been drilled right through the head like on ours.' He threaded the cord back through, knotted the snapped ends, and put it over his head so that the moth hung at his chest.

'Perhaps they were made to be worn as pendants originally,' guessed Marcia, 'when they were carved by the human species who lived here.'

'Maybe,' said Sam. 'But this cord must be a lot more recent than that. A cord that was threaded through thousands of years ago would have decayed by now.'

'Maybe the girl's parents found it and threaded this cord through, so their daughter could wear it,' suggested Zara.

'Doesn't look like they're archaeologists then,' said Ben, 'or surely they'd have wanted to check this carving out properly, rather than let their four-year-old kid run round with it.'

'That's true,' said Marcia. 'But we just don't have enough information to work any of this out. Let's get going along that cave tunnel and find the girl.'

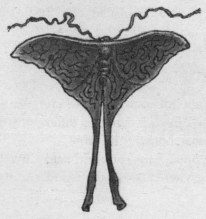

24

'We should just use one torch where we can,' suggested Zara as they set off into the tunnel, 'and save the other torch in case the first one's batteries run out.'

'Good thinking,' said Sam, switching his off.

A few bends on from where Zara and Sam had turned back before, they reached a junction where the tunnel split into two different possible routes, both narrow.

'Which way?' said Marcia, peering into both tunnels, but seeing and hearing nothing along either.

'We might as well try this way first,' suggested Zara, picking the right-hand way.

'Hang on a sec,' said Ben. He found a loose stone and scratched a crude arrow on the floor, pointing back the way they'd just come. 'So we can remember which is the way out,' he said.

They had only gone a little way along the right-hand  tunnel when it split again, this time into three options. Ben scrawled another arrow to show their way back and then they tried each tunnel in turn. The first led to a dead end; the other two led to further junctions, each of which in turn led to more splits.

'This is hopeless,' said Zara. 'This cave tunnel system is like a giant labyrinth. It must have been formed by some weird natural process, like a volcano or something. It could spread for miles. And it's impossible to know which way the girl might have gone.'

'Yeah,' said Marcia. 'And the further in we go, the more complicated it's going to be to get back. Even with Ben's arrows, there's a real risk we could get lost down here and never find our way out. I'd suggest turning back now, except we can't leave the girl down here.'

They called for the girl again, but all they heard back were their own words, echoing through the tunnel network.

'She must be seriously lost by now,' said Ben. 'No one could find their way through these caves without a map.'

Then Sam was hit by a brainwave, a theory triggered by Ben's last words. 'The moon moth pendant!' he exclaimed. 'What if the lined pattern on the wings is actually a map? A map of the cave tunnels.'

The others looked at him sceptically, and Sam realised how unlikely his idea sounded – more a leap of imagination than a properly thought-through theory. But he pressed on. 'I've just realised what those lined patterns have been reminding me of since Wilfred showed us the first moth-wing carving: a railway map – the complicated kind you see, which show all the branch lines in a rail network. If I'm right, then all the grooved lines on the moth wings represent these cave tunnels, and the map shows how they connect with each other at the junctions. We can see from the carvings back there that the human species who lived on this island used these caves. They must have needed to carve maps like this to find their way through the tunnels.' He switched his torch back on and closely examined the moon moth pendant, noticing something he hadn't spotted before. 'Look,' he said, holding it out for the others to see. 'You can see how someone's marked a continuous line right through the pattern with a pencil or something, from one side of the wings to the other.'

He was right. The pencilling was faint, just slightly greyer than the black of the jet, but visible now that Sam had pointed it out. 'That must have been done quite recently,' Sam guessed. 'If my theory's right, then the girl's parents, or whoever she's with, must have twigged that the lines were a map, then pencilled in the route through these tunnels to make the map easier to use. And then the girl must have taken the moth pendant to explore the caves by herself.'

'But I don't see how a four-year-old could possibly follow a map as complicated as this, even with the route marked,' said Zara.

'You're right,' admitted Sam. 'Maybe she's a lot older than I thought, and just small for her age. I never really got a proper look at her, even in the cave back there.'

'Well, we can test if the pattern on this moth carving is a map of these caves,' said Ben. 'If it is, then one edge of the pattern or the other ought to match up with the tunnels we've been along and junctions we've passed since entering the cave from outside.'

Adam had been studying the carved pattern intently without speaking for some moments. 'I don't think the lines on this edge match the tunnels we've been down,' he said, pointing to the moth's right wings. 'But I think the ones on the left-hand side do. Look, this single line comes in from the left-hand edge. That could be the first tunnel from the outside. Then it widens into a blob. That could be the cave chamber. Then there's a line for the second tunnel, which splits into two. And the right-hand one – the one we took – splits into three: one a dead end; and two which split off, again into the correct number of tunnels. We're just here, by this junction.'

There was a silence while everyone took this in.

'Adam's right,' said Ben. 'So Sam's theory must be correct. That's surely too many matching junctions for it to be a coincidence.'

'You're a genius, Sam!' said Marcia. 'Now we can follow the map to catch up with the girl, or follow it all the way to where the map ends at the edge of the moth. Maybe that will bring us out near the place her parents are camped.'

'Well, we should certainly try it,' said Zara. 'We need to go back to the last junction don't we, to get back on the pencilled-in route? Come on. But I think Ben should carry on drawing arrow markers at each junction, in case the map stops making sense or in case we lose our place on it.'

'Good idea,' said Sam, as they headed back to the last junction. 'It's certainly going to be hard to keep track of where we are. Every time I take my eyes of the map, I lose the place I was looking at. You could probably manage it better, Adam, with your amazing brain and memory.'

'I'll try,' said Adam, taking the moth pendant from Sam and hanging it round his neck, and borrowing Sam's torch too. 'We need to go left at this fork coming up, and we'll be back on the pencilled route.'

They took the turning, and set off along the new tunnel.

'Won't the girl get lost now that she doesn't have this map?' worried Marcia. 'She might already have taken a wrong turn and be wandering along any of the tunnels we're passing.'

'That's a point,' said Zara. 'But I can't think of anything we can do about it, except for shouting for her at every junction we get to, and looking out for her torchlight beam. But maybe she's done this route so many times that she knows it from memory, and we'll find her at the other end – wherever that is.'

Sam hoped Zara was right. It was horrible to think of the girl being lost down here, especially since it was he who'd frightened her, and he who'd grabbed the map pendant from her. But if she *could* manage to remember this route, he thought, she must definitely be older than he'd guessed.

They were travelling through the vast labyrinth, with junctions continuing to occur every thirty metres or so, and continuing to match the junctions on the moth pendant map.

'The map's not to scale,' observed Adam. 'The relative lengths of the lines between junctions don't seem to match the relative lengths of the actual tunnels. But I don't suppose it needs to be to scale for the map to work.'

'No,' agreed Ben. 'As long as the junctions are right, the map does its job. The London Tube map's the same.'

Their course had begun to take them steadily uphill. In general, the tunnel floors were smooth and easy to walk on, but from time to time their route took them over steep and rugged rock formations, which meant a difficult scramble.

Ben checked his compass regularly, and although their course meandered a bit, he was pretty sure that they were generally heading northwards. This direction of travel, he knew, must be taking them towards the centre of the island. Every turn in their complex course brought with it the sight of strange and dramatic rock formations, which cast eerie shadows in the light of their torches.

The further they went into the cave system, the more uneasy Zara felt. Partly it was a feeling of claustrophobia from being so far underground, in such confined spaces, with so much rock between them and the open sky.

And partly it was a feeling of uncertainty. Would they find the girl and whatever adults had brought her to the island? Could they really be sure these people would be safe to approach just because they had a child with them? And what was happening to the adults on board the *Pelican Queen* in the meantime? Were they even still alive?

But alongside all these definable feelings, she had another, more eerie feeling that was harder to pin down – the feeling she'd had ever since they'd arrived at the island, stronger than ever down here in the caves: the feeling that they had entered a place in which they did not belong.

They had been travelling for about twenty minutes when Adam stated that they were near the end of the map. 'The next tunnel forking off to the right should corre-spond to the line going off the right-hand edge of the moth pendant,' he said.

'You'd think that the end of the map would mark another exit from the caves,' said Marcia, 'but I can't see any sign of daylight up ahead.'

'No,' said Sam, 'but maybe there are a lot more turns and corners to come in the last two tunnels before we— Hey! Look there! The girl!'

They had just rounded a bend and there, a long way ahead, was the girl. She seemed to have some sort of torch, but it was very dim, casting the faintest of glows. All they could see of the girl was a dark silhouette, only discernible from the shadows because she was moving. She was limping – due to the ankle injury she'd sustained from her fall into the crevice, Sam guessed. He realised that this was why they'd been able to catch up with her now, in spite of her considerable head-start.

For a second, no one was sure if they should call out to her, or try to get closer before risking startling her again. But it immediately became obvious that she was aware of them anyway, for she instantly started to hobble much faster.

'Wait!' called Zara as they rushed along the tunnel after her. 'We're not going to harm you!'

But the girl vanished, her dim light going out as she seemed to merge into the shadowy rocks of the right-hand wall of the tunnel.

They quickly reached the point where she'd disappeared and scanned the tunnel wall with their torches.

There's a crack here,' said Sam, finding a narrow triangular opening in the wall. It looked big enough for a person to squeeze through, but only just. He wasn't sure they'd even have noticed it if it hadn't been for the girl.

'Come on,' said Zara, starting to make her way through. 'It could be that last tunnel marked on the map, or it could be just a cranny leading nowhere, but it must be the way she went.'

The crack took them into a cramped passageway. After several twists and turns, it emerged into an underground cavern.

The children gasped as they entered and looked around.

The cavern was enormous. Absolutely enormous. Its ceiling arced to a height of at least sixty metres, and its far side looked to be several hundred metres away. But it was not simply the size of the space that made them gasp. The cavern was filled with the ruins of a city.

25

The children gazed through the stone ruins, a chaotic jumble of collapsed buildings, broken walls, scattered blocks, toppled pillars, incomplete arches, and rubble.

Sam wondered how it was that they could see across the whole vast space, way beyond the range of their torches. Then he saw that a little daylight was coming through small openings in the cavern ceiling. However, these openings didn't give them a view of the sky above; the narrow rock shafts clearly followed an indirect route to the surface. This gave the light in the cavern a dim, diffused quality.

Even in its ruined state, the city was awe-inspiring. The scale of the buildings was immense – many had clearly been several storeys high – but it was the

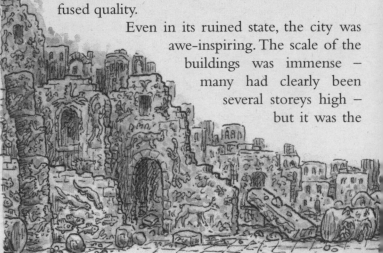

details that were most impressive. Almost every inch of every surface of every part of every stone structure had been intricately carved.

The carvings were similar in style to those they'd seen earlier around the tunnel entrance, but much, much more extensive. They depicted wildlife of every local species imaginable: hornbills, snakes, frogs, wild pigs, turtles, dragonflies, pangolins, monitor lizards. Flocks of stone parrots and swirls of stone swifts had been carved to look as if they were spiralling around columns. Troops of stone monkeys and gibbons clambered up corners of buildings. Shoals of stone fish flitted across the bases of walls, pursued by stone otters. Flying squirrels and lizards had been rendered gliding over archways. Clouded leopards had been captured mid-pounce, dropping down the sides of doorways onto deer. Even the flagstones paving the floors of the ruined buildings had been decorated with carved beetles, carved millipedes and carved armies of ants.

And most common among all the sculpted creatures of the city, often placed in prominent places at the tops of arches or above doorways, were carvings of moon moths.

'This is incredible,' said Zara. 'The people that lived on this island didn't just sit in caves making a few carvings.

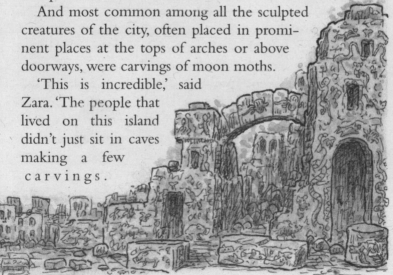

They built a city! This extinct human species developed a civilisation! And no one's ever known about it.'

'The girl must have known about this place though,' said Ben, 'from the way she knew to go through that last narrow passage. Looks like she was making for here all the time.'

'So her parents probably know about this ruined city, too,' said Sam. 'Maybe they're somewhere nearby. But I can't even see the girl.'

They all scanned the ruins, but couldn't spot the girl, or anyone else, anywhere.

'There are thousands of places she could hide around here,' observed Marcia.

'There!' said Adam suddenly.

The others looked to where he was pointing, and saw the girl, some distance away. She was still moving away from them, heading into the ruined city, clambering over the rubble of a collapsed building. She was hobbling really badly now.

'Wait! Please!' called Marcia, as they all rushed after her.

The girl continued clambering, clearly attempting to go faster. But suddenly, her ankle seemed to give way completely and she went tumbling down the rubble to the ground.

For a moment, Zara feared she'd knocked herself out or worse, but as they drew near to where the girl had come to rest they could hear her crying. She was lying on her front with her face in her hands, so that all they could see of her head was her dishevelled fair hair (her hat having been thrown off by the fall). Her shoulders shook from her sobs.

'We're really sorry,' said Zara, kneeling down beside the girl to comfort her. 'We weren't trying to frighten you. Are you badly hurt?'

The girl let out a long wobbly breath and, as if finally resigned to the fact that they'd caught up with her, she slowly sat up and raised her head to meet Zara's gaze.

As she saw the girl's face for the first time, Zara felt a wave of shock hit her in the stomach. She felt her skin tingle all over, and felt every hair on her body stand up.

The lower half of the girl's face was remarkably delicate, with a small chin, mouth and nose. These features seemed out of all proportion to her eyes. Her eyes were much bigger than any human eyes Zara had ever seen, and perfectly circular. With their huge, dark pupils and irises, they looked like the eyes of some nocturnal animal such as a bushbaby or tarsier. And beneath the skin of the girl's forehead, unmissable even in torchlight, were two slightly raised, widely spaced parallel ridges, starting just above her eyebrows and running up onto her cranium.

26

Zara tried to form words in her dry mouth. 'You're . . . you're . . .' she gasped, but neither her tongue nor vocal cords were working properly.

Sam, Adam, Ben and Marcia were similarly stunned, but Sam managed to speak. 'You're a member of the species who lived on this island!' he uttered. '*You're still here! Still alive! But—*'

'*GET AWAY FROM HER!*' A voice cut across Sam's,  making everyone jump. The voice sounded boyish in pitch, and slightly whispery in tone, but ferocious in expression. They looked upwards, in the direction from which the voice had come. They saw a figure standing at the top of the rubble that the girl had been attempting to climb, keeping himself partly concealed behind what remained of the building's wall. The figure was taller than the girl, but of a similarly slim build. His facial features were obscured by the shadowy darkness, but they could just make out that he, too, had enormous dark eyes.

Adam started to raise Sam's torch, his hand shaking.

'*Switch your torches off!*' cried the newcomer. His voice sounded intense and angry, but also desperate and nervous. '*Get away from her, and don't come any closer to me, or I—I'll kill you. I'm armed. Get away from both of us and get out of here—now! Go back to where you came from!'*

Adam and Zara turned off the two torches and the five children started to edge away, their hearts racing with shock and fear. But something made Zara wonder whether the newcomer was really armed. He'd sounded hesitant, and sounded as scared as they were. And she could see that he was not much taller than herself. She had the impression he was just a boy.

'Look,' she said, trying with difficulty to keep her voice calm, 'we'll go if that's what you want. But we mean you no harm. We were just trying to help the girl. She's hurt her ankle. We're sorry – we didn't mean to frighten her.'

'*Don't lie!*' he retorted. 'She wouldn't have fallen if you hadn't been chasing her. I know you were trying to catch her. That's what you've come to this island to do – catch us or kill us. Now *leave*. You're lucky I'm letting you go.'

'Do what he says,' said a new voice. 'Leave now and forget you ever saw us.' This voice was low and husky, though somehow feminine, and sounded cracked with age. It came from the shadows of a nearby ruined archway, where it was too dark for them even to glimpse the speaker.

Marcia found she was trembling all over. She looked around, wondering how many more of these people were hiding in the ruins, watching them. Part of her wanted to turn and run away. But part of her knew that they had to stay and find out more about who these people were. 'But we can't forget we ever saw you!' she said. 'And we didn't come here to catch or kill anyone! We didn't know that anyone was still living here – didn't know that any people like you still existed!'

'*Lies!*' shouted the boyish figure. 'You've known all about us for *months!* Admit it! We know that it was your colleague, Sebastian Speerling, who killed our uncle, a year ago, in Italy.'

'*Sebastian Speerling?*' echoed Marcia. 'We don't know *anyone* called Sebastian Speerling.'

'More lies! We know he joined you the night before last, in Malaysia. We know he came here with you yesterday. You're working with him.'

'You must mean the person we knew as Simon Arblinton!' exclaimed Ben, suddenly realising they had been wrong to think that Simon's impostor had merely been after a five-thousand-year-old skeleton and artefacts. 'So he knew that you people were living here all along!' He took a step forward. 'Please believe us,' he implored the figure. 'This Sebastian Speerling tricked us. He pretended to be someone else – an archaeologist – and latched himself onto our expedition. We didn't know anything about his real plans. We still don't, not properly. I'm sorry he killed your uncle. He tried to kill us, too – shot our plane down yesterday evening. We're stranded here.'

There was a pause. Then, for the first time, the girl spoke. She spoke not in English, but in a strange language, fast-flowing and full of breathy, hissing sounds.

After she stopped there was another pause, and then the older feminine voice spoke again from the archway. 'The girl says that she does not think you were going to harm her,' said the unseen speaker, sounding slightly less hostile, but still wary. 'She tells me she ran from you to avoid being seen, not because you were being aggressive. And that after she hurt her ankle, you were only trying to help her. And we did hear an explosion yesterday evening, so maybe you are telling the truth about Sebastian Speerling shooting down your plane. But even if you are not working with him, you have done great damage by bringing him to this island. Now go.'

'But we should help each other!' said Sam. 'Sebastian's killed your uncle and, from what you say, your people are in danger from him. And he's drugged the adults who were with us and flown off with them. We all need to find him and stop him. We need to contact the authorities and—'

'No!' interrupted the boyish figure. '*Your* conflict with Sebastian has got nothing to do with us. You *Homo sapiens* people are *always* tricking each other and harming each other and killing each other. It's what your species does; you should be used to it. And your authorities can be of no help to *us*. To them, we don't exist, and that's the way it must stay. We want nothing to do with your species. We'll defend ourselves from Sebastian in our own way.'

By now, the children had backed some distance away from the girl. Suddenly, the boyish figure emerged from his semi-concealment and, moving with impressive speed and agility, rushed down the rubble, scooped the girl up with an arm, and carried her into the shadows of a nearby building.

This brief but clearer view of him confirmed Zara's impression that he was a boy rather than a man – a boy of about fourteen years old, judging by his height and general proportions. He had short, dark brown hair and wore a black T-shirt, fawn trousers and jungle boots. He didn't appear to be armed, Zara noticed. In addition to his big eyes, he had the other distinctive features that the girl had – the small lower face and the two head ridges. Zara also noticed that, like the skeleton in the other cave, the boy and the girl both had rather long arms.

The boy had all but disappeared with the girl into their new hiding place when the girl began speaking again, still in her own language, but more forcefully this time. Then the boy and the unseen older woman could also be heard speaking, this time using the same language as the girl. It seemed to Zara that the three of them were arguing.

Eventually, the woman's voice spoke in English once more, addressing the five *Homo sapiens* children now. 'The girl believes we should trust you. Her older brother believes strongly that we should not. Under normal circumstances, I would agree with him. But these are not normal circumstances.' Walking slowly, the speaker emerged from the archway.

26

The woman was lean and tall, though she walked with a slightly stooped posture. Her pale-brown face – which shared the same non-*Homo sapiens* features as the boy and girl – was deeply wrinkled and framed by grey hair. Her clothes looked less modern and ordinary than the boy's and girl's. She wore a loose turquoise robe, and sandals on her feet.

From his hiding place in the shadows, the boy's voice spoke up once more, speaking fast in their strange language, and still sounding angry. But the woman held up her hand authoritatively, stopping the boy in what sounded like mid-sentence.

'Firstly, Marno,' she said, 'let us all speak in English. There is enough confusion in this situation already without putting up unnecessary language barriers between ourselves and our uninvited visitors. And secondly, yes I am fully aware of the Great Rule. I have been following it and teaching it to children like you for my whole long life. Of *course* I shouldn't be showing myself to these *Homo sapiens* people. But *you've* already shown *yourself*. And so has your sister Embie before that. So it is somewhat late to stick to the rule now, is it not? Come out of there and join us over here.'

The boy re-emerged from his hiding place, still carrying

the girl. He came to a halt behind the old woman, glowering with hostility.

'Now,' said the old woman, looking at the five intruders with some suspicion herself. 'How did you find your way into here?'

'I saw the girl, Embie,' said Sam. 'Outside, in the rainforest. We followed her into the caves. Then she lost her moth pendant. Well, actually I grabbed it, but accidentally. We worked out that the lines on the moth carving were a map of the cave tunnels and used it to follow her here. We were worried she'd get lost. We wanted to help her and we thought she must be on the island with adults who could help us.'

'I'm sure he's telling the truth,' said the girl to the old woman, speaking in English for the first time. 'It was my fault for letting them see me. I shouldn't have been outside on my own. I know you told us not to, but I didn't know it was dangerous. Marno said just now that the man who killed Uncle Azlo is here, but you never told me that, so I didn't know. I just wanted to go out to watch the gibbons like we used to do in the mornings. I went across the city and out through the tunnels by myself. And then, in the forest, I saw these people. I only had a little look at them. I thought they wouldn't see me, but they did. I'm really, really sorry. I tried to get away from them. I didn't mean to lead them back here.' She clung to her brother and looked as if she might start crying again.

'Do not be too hard on yourself,' said the old woman, sighing and giving the girl a comforting pat. 'It's not your fault for wanting to go outside. Marno and I guessed you must have gone to watch the gibbons when we found you gone this morning. That's why we were coming this way looking for you. I should have made my warning not to go out more forceful. I should have told you more, but I was trying to avoid frightening you. Anyway,' she added, speaking slowly now and clearly thinking hard, 'what's happened has happened. And maybe some good can come out of your accidental encounter with these children. It goes against everything I have always believed and practised, but I am wondering if this is an occasion when we should accept help from members of the *Homo sapiens* species, since these children have seen us anyway. You say that we will defend ourselves from Sebastian Speerling in our own way, Marno, but the truth is, we have very few defences, and he is an extremely dangerous enemy.' She looked hard at the five children. 'You say that you knew nothing of Sebastian Speerling and his plans – that he was pretending to be someone else and using your expedition for his own ends without your knowledge; that he drugged the adults in your group and tried to kill you as you escaped. Is that the absolute truth?'

'Yes!' said Marcia. 'We *promise* that's the truth.'

The others all forcefully attested to this.

'Our expedition was purely scientific,' said Ben, 'to investigate an ancient skeleton that had been found here years ago by our friend Wilfred.'

'We honestly had no idea that people like you were still living,' said Sam.

'And we promise never to reveal your existence to any-one if you don't want us to,' said Zara.

'We'll do anything we can to help you against Sebastian, whatever he's planning,' added Adam.

Without speaking, the woman continued to look at them for several more seconds, and the children could almost *feel* her taking in everything about them through the huge black pupils of her enormous eyes.

'It is almost unheard of for us to trust members of your species,' said the woman at last, 'but it seems the time has come when I must do so, and I feel in my heart that my trust in you will not be misplaced. So, thank you for your offer of help. I promise that we, in return, will do everything we can to help rescue your adult companions. My name is Antha. Embie and Marno's names you know already.'

The five *Homo sapiens* children introduced themselves. Marno remained sullenly silent, holding Embie protectively.

'Now, let us begin with the most urgent matter,' said Antha. 'Do you know where Sebastian is now?'

'We heard him taking off in our big flying boat yesterday evening,' said Ben, 'shortly after he'd shot us down. We thought he was leaving the island for good, but that was before we knew you were here and that he was trying to track you down. Maybe he's just gone off to get more equipment or reinforcements.'

'We should assume that he will be back,' agreed the woman grimly. 'But if he has flown away for now, that gives us a bit of time to think and plan.'

'Do you have some sort of radio, or a satellite phone system?' asked Zara. 'We could contact the Malaysian authorities. We wouldn't need to tell anybody about you – we could say we radioed from our crashed plane. If the Malaysian navy or air force could find the *Pelican Queen*, rescue the adults and arrest Sebastian for kidnapping, that would solve all our problems.'

'Such a plan may be possible,' agreed Antha, 'as long as we are sure it can be achieved without jeopardising our secrecy. Come, let us lose no more time.' She turned and began making her way through the ruins, following the same direction as the girl had when she'd fallen. 'I will need to take you to our home,' she said, 'on the other side of this ancient city. As we go, I will try to give you some explanations about who we are and why we are living here.'

28

'It must be strange for you to discover that you are not the only human species on the planet,' said Antha.

Strange was an understatement. The five children – the five *Homo sapiens* children – were still in a state of mind-reeling shock. Their brains were racing with questions. How many of these people were there? Had they ever lived alongside *Homo sapiens*, or had they always lived in hiding? Why did they live so secretly?

'I'll begin my explanation at the beginning,' Antha continued. 'Way, way back in time, millions of years ago, we must have shared a common ancestor with your species, but at some stage we branched off from your evolutionary line, settled in this part of the world, and evolved quite differently from you. We evolved to be leaner, lighter and more agile than *Homo sapiens*, better able to move through the rainforest trees. And whereas your species followed the trend of most apes to be daytime creatures, *we* gradually evolved to be most active at night. Our own name for our species translates into your language as 'The Night People'. I suppose that means that your scientists would categorise us as *Homo nocturnus*.

'Possibly our evolution into becoming nocturnal was driven by a need to avoid competition with other human species, such as yours. Your species seems to have always had an aggressive, warlike side. Our species is naturally shyer and less aggressive, usually preferring to hide when challenged, rather than fight.

'Our two species are different in many other ways, too. Your species likes to organise itself into tribes, with everyone in the tribe being expected to follow the same leader, the same religious beliefs and the same social customs. This seems almost as true of your modern nations as it was of your Stone Age settlements. Our species, on the other hand, tends to live in groups which have no leader, where people work together only if they want to, and where people's beliefs and thoughts are entirely personal.'

'Your way sounds better,' said Marcia.

'But *Homo sapiens* became the more successful species,' Antha pointed out. 'Your ancestors' forceful, highly organised behaviour enabled them to grow their populations and spread out from Africa to every part of the world. Our ancestors remained local to Southeast Asia. And, because we have a naturally low birth rate compared to your species, our population level remained relatively small.

'The fossil evidence of our species' prehistory now lies beyond the reach of archaeologists. This whole region was once a vast subcontinent, but like other parts of the world, it was flooded by a series of sudden rises in sea level at the end of the last Ice Age. The last of these cataclysmic floods occurred around eight thousand years ago, forming the South China Sea and leaving only the peninsulas and islands we see today.

'The members of our species who survived the flood seem to have done so by establishing themselves on this island. Here, our ancestors lived in peaceful isolation from *Homo sapiens* for the next three thousand years. Here, in this vast underground cavern in the centre of the island, they built this city. The oldest parts were built around seven thousand years ago; the most recent parts, just over five thousand years ago.'

Sam noticed that the walls of the cavern also had windows, doorways and animal carvings in them. He wondered if the city had started in the cavern walls, as clusters of cave dwellings, then grown out into the space, as the Night People had constructed more and more buildings. The city certainly looked as if its architects had been making things up as they went along, adding bits to buildings here and there as needed, rather than working to some grand geometric master plan. He also noticed that features such as doors and archways had been built to a practical, human scale rather than to the grandiose proportions you saw in pictures of ancient Rome or Egypt.

'Here on the island', continued Antha, 'our ancestors developed a civilisation that, in many aspects of culture and technology, was more advanced than the *Homo sapiens* civilisations of the same era.'

Marcia tried to imagine what the city would have looked like back then, when its buildings were intact and its streets were bustling with activity. It was hard to envisage. The whole ruined city was as still and silent as a graveyard. Apart from themselves, there was not a living soul to be seen.

So far, Antha's route through the city had stuck to the relatively flat ground level of the cavern, which had meant an easy walk over the remains of ancient paving stones. But now a sprawling complex of ruined buildings completely blocked their way, and, rather than trying to find a way round, Antha led them over it instead, over heaps of rubble, mounds of broken pillars, and up the steep slopes of collapsed walls. They had to go single file, which meant that Antha had to break off her talk for a while.

Antha negotiated the obstacles with remarkable ease, as did Marno, even though he was still carrying Embie, who was now sitting on his shoulders. But the others struggled to keep up as they scrambled over the broken masonry.

Then Antha led them down through the middle of the ruined buildings. Inside, stone ceilings blocked out the diffused daylight of the cavern, and Sam and Zara had to switch on their torches. Sam noticed that Antha, Marno and Embie switched on tiny lamps which were clipped to their collars – simple translucent spheres, no bigger than marbles, which emitted a very dim amber glow. Clearly that was enough light for the Night People to find their way. Sam guessed that their peculiarly big eyes must somehow enable them to see in near-darkness.

Eventually, they emerged from an archway on the other side of the buildings, back into the grey light of the cavern, and were soon walking on flat ground once more.

'Do you want me to take a turn at carrying Embie?' Marcia asked Marno, wanting to be helpful.

Embie gave Marcia a smile, but Marno scowled. 'She's *my* sister,' he said curtly. 'I'll carry her.'

Marcia shrugged, unable to think of a way to make Marno trust or like them.

By now, they were in the middle of the city. Antha led them onwards and continued her explanation.

29

'Although our ancestors built this city underground,' said Antha, 'they also used the rest of the island – the rainforest and the coast. They used the network of cave tunnels to get from the city to other places on the island. And, as you have already deduced it seems, they carved maps onto pendants so they could find their way. The black moon moth, nocturnal and unique to this island, was a favourite symbol of our ancestors, so perhaps it is not surprising that they used its shape for this important purpose.'

Adam remembered that he was still wearing Embie's moon moth pendant. 'Here,' he said, returning it to her. 'You'd better have this back.'

'Thank you,' she said, putting the cord around her neck. 'It's Antha's really. But she lets me wear it because she knows her way around the tunnels without it. So does Marno.'

'So did you just now,' Ben pointed out. 'You found your way back here after you lost it.'

'I didn't know I could do that until I tried,' said Embie.

'I suppose I have been along that tunnel many times before.'

'Still pretty impressive though,' said Ben. Although Embie seemed to be a few years older than Sam had first guessed, she was still only a young child.

'Our brains are good at remembering routes,' said Antha. 'And also, we seem to have a slight natural ability to sense the earth's magnetic field and know where north and south are. You can see from the shape of our craniums that our brains have evolved quite differently from yours. Our ancestors probably didn't need to use the pendant maps every time they used the tunnels either. But they may have carried them for safety, or for using in tunnels they were less familiar with. We believe there must have been differently patterned pendants for each of the different tunnel systems. However, the only surviving pendants we have are for the only two tunnel systems that remain unblocked today: the one you followed Embie through this morning, and one that comes up from some sea-caves near the bay.'

'We found another moth pendant in a different cave,' Ben told her, 'next to the skeleton I mentioned earlier.'

He told Antha the story of how Wilfred had first discovered the skeleton, and he described the location of the cave.

'I know the cave you mean,' she said. 'I have never noticed there was a skeleton under the rocks, or we would have excavated the cave ourselves, but from what you say the bones were well covered up when your friend first found them, and again by subsequent rockfalls.'

'So do you think that cave was linked to this city by underground tunnels?' asked Marcia.

'If a moth pendant was found there, it seems likely,' said

Antha. 'As I said, we believe there were once many tunnel systems leading out from this city, before they collapsed, along with the city itself.'

'What happened?' asked Zara. 'How did this whole city become ruined and deserted?'

'An earthquake,' said Antha. 'A massive earthquake which hit the island just over five thousand years ago. It's all recorded on stone tablets that were engraved by the survivors not long after the event. The earthquake shook the city to pieces within minutes, and many of its inhabitants were killed outright. Most of those who were still alive tried to flee through the tunnel systems. But the earthquake caused almost all of these tunnels to collapse, and the people using them were crushed in the rock-falls.'

'So the skeleton Wilfred found could have been someone who'd been trying to escape the earthquake,' said Marcia. 'Someone who'd used the moth pendant to find their way along that tunnel. And they must have thought they'd made it. They were only a few metres from the mouth of the cave.' It was a horrible thing to think about.

'What happened after the earthquake?' asked Zara. 'You said that there were some survivors left who recorded the event.'

'Yes, there were some survivors,' said Antha. 'They tried to clear up the rubble and bury the dead. But then they were hit by a disease, probably caused by bodies polluting the underground streams that were the city's water supply. Even after they moved away from the ruined city to the edges of the island, the disease spread quickly through the already weakened population, killing many. Those who remained alive made a decision. Rather than stay to die slowly, they would leave the island. They got into their small fishing boats, taking the minimum of possessions, and sailed off across the sea to the outside world.'

30

'Our ancestors were extremely wary of your species,' continued Antha. 'During the previous three thousand years, the time before the earthquake, *Homo sapiens* sailors had occasionally come to the island to stock up on meat, fruit and water. Whenever this happened, our ancestors had hidden in their underground city until the visitors left, avoiding showing themselves at all.

'And this was the policy they adopted now that they were entering a world ruled by *Homo sapiens*. They saw the violence that members of your species were capable of inflicting on one another. They saw how your tribes or nations would often attempt to wipe out other tribes or nations, simply because they were different from themselves. If *Homo sapiens* people reacted like this to slightly different members of their own species, how would they treat people from a different species altogether?

'So our ancestors sought out the earth's most isolated

places, where they could live invisibly in peace and safety. Over the last five thousand years, our species has dispersed around the whole world, with small pockets of us living in most countries. In the last few centuries, it has become more and more difficult to find isolated places that are beyond the gaze of your species. So during this time, many of our species have moved into your big cities, finding disused spaces where they can live their nocturnal lifestyle. It seems the one type of habitat where your species doesn't notice what or who is around them is a big city. Of course, these city-dwellers have needed to wear headgear or disguises that conceal their distinctive features whenever they go out. And they have had to be careful of standing in postures that would draw attention to their slightly different proportions. You five may have passed members of our species in the streets of London or Edinburgh, without ever knowing it.'

Zara found this a very odd thing to think about. In fact she found everything about these people very odd to think about. It wasn't the fact that they looked so different from ordinary humans that was making her brain spin and her stomach tingle – she was quite used to seeing people in everyday life who looked unusual in some way, and Antha, Marno and Embie's distinctive facial features had quickly ceased to be shocking. It was the revelation that a completely different species of human was sharing the planet with her own species that Zara was finding so hard to take in.

'It is because we have lived among you', continued Antha, 'that we can speak your languages so fluently. Our brains learn languages fast, and both Marno and Embie can already speak several. Occasionally, we have given a little assistance to members of your species – little hints towards scientific breakthroughs, little nudges towards the development of progressive ideas – anything to encourage your species in its uphill struggle to become more civilised. But such contributions have always been given secretly, almost invisibly.'

'But surely', said Ben, 'there must have been *some* occasions over the last five thousand years when people – I mean people of our species – have noticed people from your species and caught sight of their features.'

'Yes,' said Antha, 'there have been a few isolated encounters. But usually, anyone spotting one of us has assumed that they were simply looking at a "freak" or a "deformed" person, as they would call it. And on the very rare occasions when a whole group of us have been glimpsed, living in a forest or fleeing into a cave, accounts of such sightings have been dismissed as folk myths. So the secret of our species' existence has remained virtually undiscovered.'

'But have some of you come back to live on this island now?' asked Sam.

'A few of us live here,' said Antha. 'During the centuries following the earthquake, as our species dispersed across the world, we forgot much of our own history. This island became almost a place of myth, rather than reality. But about a thousand years ago, some members of our species began to research our history properly. They rediscovered the island, which was still uninhabited, they rediscovered the two unblocked tunnel systems, and they rediscovered the city. They found the stone tablets I mentioned, which had been left to record what had happened. It was decided that a small group of them would stay here on the island as permanent guardians of our ancestral home. It was also decided that, every forty years, all known groups of our species across the world would send representatives to the island for a gathering.

'This tradition has continued ever since, with at least two members of our species living here as guardians of the island at all times. I have lived here as one of the current two guardians for the last eighty-three years. My husband Ushrol, who you will meet shortly, is the other.'

'Eighty-three years?' said Marcia. 'You must have started being a guardian when you were still a child.'

'I was fifty-two,' said Antha.

'*Fifty-two!*' exclaimed Sam. '*Eighty-three years ago!* But that would make you . . .'

'One hundred and thirty-five,' said Adam, as quick as ever with the mental arithmetic.

'Quite right,' said Antha. 'Our lifespans tend to be considerably longer than those of your species. It is quite normal for us to reach one hundred and forty, and one hundred and sixty is not unknown. You should not be so surprised. Your scientists know of quite a number of animal species which have longer average lifespans than you.'

'I know,' said Zara, 'but it's weird to think of a *human* living that long.'

Marno interjected, speaking for the first time since he had refused help from Marcia. 'Yes, we must seem very weird to you generally,' he said in a bitter tone. 'Sorry we can't be more *normal* for you.'

'I didn't mean it like that!' cried Zara. 'I just meant—'

'It's all right,' said Antha. 'We know what you meant.'

'Marno doesn't really hate you,' added Embie. 'He's just sad all the time because of what happened to Uncle Azlo.'

'Don't talk to them, Embie!' ordered Marno. 'You're just a scientific specimen to them. Just another interesting discovery for them to put on their list of species to exploit, or drive to extinction.'

'Marno!' said Antha firmly. 'That is enough! I have

decided to trust these people and they are our guests.'

Marno fell quiet. He flashed another hostile glance at Zara and the others, then looked away, ignoring them altogether.

There was an awkward silence, but Sam broke it by asking Antha another question. 'How many of you are there in the world?' he said.

'That is a good question,' said Antha, 'and I will answer it shortly. But we have arrived at our home and I need to see to Embie's ankle first.'

They had reached the other side of the cavern. There were several round-arched, ornately carved doorways in this part of the cavern wall, but most looked disused and crumbling. Only one had a door in it, a solid-looking door made from dark wood. Antha took an iron key from her pocket, unlocked the door and swung it open.

31

Antha led them into a curved stone passageway, with irregularly shaped rooms leading off on either side. The stonework was ornately carved in a similar style to the city buildings outside, though on a smaller scale. The space was dimly lit by round lamps built into the designs.

'First,' said Antha, shutting and locking the door behind them, 'let me have a quick look at that ankle of yours, Embie. That's it, Marno; carry Embie to her room.'

They went into a small, simply furnished room, where Marno laid Embie down in a hammock that was suspended across the space, about a metre above the floor.

'Well done, Marno,' said Antha, speaking much more kindly to him than she had a few moments ago. 'That was a long way to carry your sister.'

'Yeah, thanks Marno,' said Embie.

'No problem,' said Marno, giving his sister a smile. He continued to ignore the other children.

Antha removed Embie's left jungle boot and examined the ankle. 'It's only slightly swollen,' she said. 'Just a minor twist. It should be better after a good day's sleep. Now, we must get on. Marno, perhaps you could fetch Embie's toothbrush and stay with her for a bit, while I take our visitors up to see Ushrol. We will be back down shortly.'

This momentarily struck Sam as an odd time for Embie

to be going to bed, until he remembered that she belonged to a nocturnal species.

Leaving Marno to look after his sister, Antha hurried the others from the room and along the winding passageway.

'Your question about how many of us there are in the world is a pertinent one, Sam,' she said in a low voice, once they were some distance from Embie's bedroom, 'but it is not a question I wished to answer in front of Embie. She has had enough problems blighting her childhood already, and I would like to spare her knowing the full extent of our species' predicament until she is a little older. The truth is, I do not know exactly how many of us are left in the world. But I do know that our numbers are declining, and declining fast. As I said, our birth rate has always been low, but in recent decades it has fallen so drastically that the birth of a child has become a rare event. And at the same time, we have been hit, across the world, by a disease for which we can find no cure. This illness seems to be an airborne virus which we think is carried around the world by your species as well as ours. It is entirely harmless to you – your species is not even aware of it – but it weakens members of our species terribly, often causing death. Embie and Marno's parents both have the illness, and are being cared for in one of our special hospitals. That is why Embie and Marno have come to live here on the island with us, as have many other children in recent years who have needed a safe home. We do what we can to help one another, but it may not be enough. At our last island gathering, seven years ago, only a fraction of the number of representatives we have seen at previous gatherings managed to make it. And those that came all reported the same thing: a drastic decline in population numbers in their counties. Already, our worldwide population seems to have fallen to just a few thousand. From there, it could so easily fall away to zero. I fear we may be witnessing our own extinction.'

'But . . . that's *awful!*' said Ben.

'We have not given up trying to survive,' said Antha. 'But the world – the world your species controls – is becoming a harder and harder place for us to live in so many way. It is becoming increasingly difficult to function on this planet without things like biometric passports, driving licences, bank accounts and credit cards – all things that are hard to obtain when you don't officially exist. And it is becoming impossible for us to get around the planet without being noticed by all your security and surveillance measures.'

'Couldn't you all come back to live on this island?' asked Adam.

'It has been discussed,' said Antha, 'but apart from the fear of making the disease worse by concentrating ourselves in one place, there are doubts that we would all be able to remain hidden here for long. The only reason this island has remained protected as an unpopulated wildlife reserve for so long is that one of our species is an influential environmental adviser to the Malaysian government.' She smiled wryly. 'The newspapers refer to him as "a notably reclusive academic, never seen in public without the dark sunglasses which protect his weak eyes". But for how much longer will this island remain ignored and undeveloped if oil and gas are found near its shores?'

'Anyway,' she said, seeming to snap herself out of her despondency, 'the most *immediate* threat to our survival here on the island, and to your companions, is Sebastian Speerling, so let's concentrate on *that* problem for now.'

Throughout everything, the children's desperate worries about the adults on the *Pelican Queen* had, of course, remained at the front of their minds. They all kept silently

telling themselves that the adults were only unconscious and still unharmed. They couldn't allow themselves to start wondering about any worse possibilities.

They had reached the end of the passageway. Set into the wall in front of them was a deep alcove, and in it stood a big square wicker basket, similar to the basket of a hot-air balloon. 'Come on,' said Antha, stepping over its side.

Mystified, they clambered into the basket with her.

32

Antha pulled a wooden lever, a sound of clattering machinery started up, and the basket started to rise, pulled by cables at each corner. Looking up, the children saw that they were travelling steadily upwards through a tall rocky shaft. There were a couple of glimmers of daylight visible some way above them.

'Lifts were one of the many things we invented before your species did,' said Antha. 'This actual basket doesn't date back to the time of the city, of course, but the whole thing is based on the same design they used back then. It's driven by a waterwheel, powered by a nearby underground river.'

'Cool,' said Sam.

'How high are we going?' asked Adam. 'The top of this shaft looks even higher than the ceiling of the city cavern.'

'Well observed,' said Antha. 'We are indeed going beyond the height of the cavern, and up through the middle of one of the island's craggy peaks – one of the dragon's teeth, as the Malaysians call them. The twelve peaks of the island were the towers of our ancient civilisation.'

'You mean they're hollow inside?' exclaimed Ben.

'Yes,' said Antha. 'A strange natural rock formation, which our ancestors were able to take advantage of, with a bit of extra chiselling-out. Each crag had several storeys, and windows too, concealed beneath the hanging greenery you will have seen as you flew past them yesterday. They made ideal watchtowers, of course, to keep a lookout for any approaching *Homo sapiens* boats, but mostly they seem to have been used because the people liked being up high from time to time. The interiors of most of the crag towers were wrecked in the earthquake. This is the only one that remains in use.'

She pushed the lever, and the lift stopped next to an opening, some way below the top of the shaft. The children followed Antha onto a small landing. Opposite them was a tiny unglazed window, screened on the outside by a veil of ferns and vines hanging down from above.

Near to the lift alcove was a closed wooden door. 'I had better tell Ushrol about you before you come in,' said Antha before opening it. 'Wait here.'

She went through and closed the door behind her. The children could hear her voice speaking in her own language. Then they could hear another voice replying in the same language. No, there was more than one other voice. It sounded like a small group of people in there.

The children looked out of the window. Through the foliage, they had an incredible view of other nearby 'teeth' crags and the rainforest below. It was good to see the outside world again. The morning mist was still rising up through the trees, obscuring the view of the sea beyond. It seemed an age since they had been down in the forest, waking up and listening to the gibbons singing. It had, in reality, been less than a few hours, but during that time their whole understanding of the world had been changed.

Soon, Antha opened the door and beckoned them into a fairly large room with uneven rocky walls that sloped inwards towards the ceiling. From the room's width, Ben guessed they must be about halfway up the inside of the crag.

The room had a single window, larger than the one on the landing but also unglazed and similarly camouflaged from the outside. Near to it, an old man and three young men were seated round a table. They looked to be in the middle of eating a meal of fruit and fried fish, but they all stood up as the children entered. The old man looked extremely frail. He had to lean on a walking stick and the edge of the table to haul himself to his feet. His hair was white, and so wispy that his head ridges were visible over the whole dome of his cranium. The three young men  all had brown hair, and all wore black clothes.

All four men stared at the children, assessing them with their big round eyes. They looked very uneasy, but nervous rather than hostile.

'I am Ushrol,' said the old man at last in a soft, gravelly voice. 'And these three youngsters are Hal, Peplo and Ubie. They are brothers – Marno and Embie's cousins. They arrived from the Malaysian mainland just now, whilst Antha and Marno were out looking for Embie.'

The children introduced themselves, and the four men shook their hands. Hal was the biggest of the three brothers, and seemed the least timid in his manner. He had the air of being the eldest. Ubie was the smallest brother, and looked younger that the other two. Peplo had a particularly thin, serious-looking face, and he examined the newcomers with a studious expression.

'Meeting members of your species openly and face-to-face like this feels very, very strange,' said Ushrol. 'But I trust my wife's judgement, and she trusts you. It seems we have a common enemy whom we must thwart. Now, Antha says that Sebastian took off in the big flying boat yesterday evening, holding your companions prisoner, and that your plan is to send a distress message using our radio?'

'Yes,' said Zara. 'Please. If we can get a message to the Malaysian authorities, they might be able to intercept Sebastian and arrest him. It's our best hope. We wouldn't tell them about you; we promise we wouldn't. We'd say we used the radio from our small plane, which crashed in the forest. And we could get ourselves down to the beach to meet anyone coming to rescue us, so that they never saw you. But we should hurry. Sebastian could be miles away by now.'

Ushrol pondered this suggestion for a moment, then nodded. 'It is a good plan,' he agreed. 'And you are right – the quicker the better. Hal, could you lift the radio down for me, please?'

One of the room's walls had rows of shelves hollowed into it. From the piles of ornate mechanical clutter that filled the middle shelf, Hal lifted down a large metal box-like object, beautifully crafted and covered with intricate dials and tiny switches. He put it on the table in front of Ushrol, who sat down and produced a small screwdriver from his brown canvas jacket.

'We use the radio quite a lot for long-range communication,' he said, unscrewing the front of the set. 'But we use a completely different form of transmission than your species' radio systems, to avoid our messages being detected. So I am going to have to make a few changes to our set before you can try to contact anyone. It should not take me more than ten or fifteen minutes, though. Please, sit down. Share our food if you are hungry.'

'Thank you,' said Zara.

The delicious smell of the fried fish had been making them all acutely aware of how long it was since they had eaten anything. Peplo, Ubie and Hal found some more plates and chairs, and before long the children were ravenously devouring an extremely welcome breakfast. Peplo soon had to go to the stove in the corner and do some more frying.

'This is not the first time my brothers and I have met you,' remarked Hal, to the children.

The children frowned in puzzlement. What did he mean? Surely they had never met these three men before, nor anyone of their species until this morning.

'*You* were running across a car park towards us,' Ubie added, 'and *we* were fleeing into the trees.'

33

'You're the three men who attacked Simon!' exclaimed Marcia. 'I mean Sebastian.' A thought occurred to her. 'Your cousin Marno told us that Sebastian had killed his uncle,' she said. 'Was—was that your father? Is that why you were attacking Sebastian with a knife?'

'We weren't attacking him with a knife!' said Ubie, clearly outraged. 'Is that what he told you? The knife was *his*! *We* don't carry weapons. *He* tried to use it on *us*, but Peplo kicked it out of his hand.'

'I'm sorry!' said Marcia quickly. 'We shouldn't have believed anything he told us. We know that now. But he was a very good liar.'

'He even thought to pick up the knife himself afterwards,' said Adam, casting his mind back, 'to cover the fact that his fingerprints would be found on the handle.'

Quickly, Zara told their hosts the whole story of how Sebastian had infiltrated their expedition by pretending to be the young archaeologist Simon Arblinton.

'But we still don't know anything about Sebastian,' said Ben. 'Why did he kill your uncle?'

'We'd better tell you the whole story properly while Ushrol sorts out the radio,' said Antha. 'The first thing you need to know is that when I said that the secret of our species' existence has remained virtually undiscovered over the centuries, I did mean virtually — not totally. There *have* been a very few members of your species who have learned of us, the most notable of whom was a seventeenth-century Italian explorer named Giovanni di Radelfi. On his travels in India, Radelfi had somehow discovered a man of our species and, to cut a long story short, befriended him and learned the secret of the Night People. Radelfi eventually persuaded the man to take him to this island, disguised as one of us, to watch one of our forty-year gatherings. He got his friend to teach him our language, so he was able to discover a huge amount about us during his time on the island. He promised his friend that he would never tell another living soul about us. He may have kept his word, but he couldn't resist writing a personal journal of his secret expedition to the island. He wrote it in a cipher of his own devising and never published it or showed it to anyone. Some years later, the guardians of the island found out what had happened, but by then Radelfi had died, back in his home city of Bologna, and his journal had  been lost amongst his dispersed possessions. Since then, our people in Europe always kept an eye out for the journal, knowing that it could, if deciphered, reveal our entire existence and the location of our ancestral island. But the journal never showed up.'

'Until a year ago,' said Hal, taking up the story, 'when our father, Azlo, who had a great love of books — books by your species and ours — happened to spot that Radelfi's journal was on sale in an antiquarian bookshop in Rome. It was listed in their online catalogue. It hadn't been deciphered and was being sold as an antique curiosity.'

'Italy is where we lived,' explained Ubie. 'Until last year, we lived with our father in a hidden loft apartment above an old warehouse in the port of Genoa. Our mother died some years ago.'

'Anyway,' said Hal, 'using money pooled by members of our species, our father was able to purchase Radelfi's journal. The plan was for it to be brought here to the island to be kept safe for ever. However, unbeknown to any of us, someone else had also been on the trail of the book – a young scientist called Sebastian Speerling. We don't know where Sebastian first heard rumours about the existence of our species or the existence of Radelfi's journal. Maybe Radelfi had told other people after all, and the rumours had spread down the centuries; or maybe there was another source. What we do know is that Sebastian had been looking for the long-lost journal for some time. He, too, must have spotted its appearance on the book dealer's website. He travelled to the shop in Rome from his home in London, only to find that our father had just beaten him to it. So he secretly followed him, trailing him back to our home in Genoa.'

'When our father came home with the journal', said Peplo, 'we stayed up all day with him, cracking Radelfi's cipher so that we could read the journal. Our brains are good at that sort of thing.' He sighed. 'It was a good day, the last we spent with him. The following night, Sebastian broke into our apartment and tried to steal the journal. My father burst in on him and tried to stop him, but Sebastian had a knife and stabbed him. We came running from another room and Sebastian fled. In the scuffle before the stabbing, the book had got torn in two and Sebastian got away with only half the pages of the journal. Our father died instantly from the stab wound.'

34

The three brothers stared down at the table for a few moments without speaking. Then Hal continued. 'It took months of detective work to find out who our father's killer was, and a lot of travelling to find out *where* he was. We weren't after revenge – we don't have it in us to kill people – but we had to find out how much he knew, and what he was doing.'

'Just a few days ago', said Peplo, 'we finally discovered that he was in Thailand. It turned out that he'd been in Southeast Asia for a while, trying to track down the location of our ancient underground city. He'd quickly cracked Radelfi's cipher, but his problem was that he didn't have the whole journal. The only pages that he'd got were from the latter half of Radelfi's account, describing his observations of the people attending the gathering, and details of the city. These pages didn't describe the location of the city, or even refer to the fact that it was on an island. Radelfi's account of travelling here was in the earlier pages, which we still had. Sebastian was able to deduce that the location was in Southeast Asia from Radelfi's descriptions of the local wildlife, but that was all he knew.'

'So he'd been travelling around the archaeological sites of this region for a year,' said Ubie, 'trying to pick up rumours of any place where odd remains had been found, remains that might match Radelfi's descriptions. As Peplo said, we caught up with him in Thailand, at an archaeological dig at the site of a temple.'

'Where he must have met the real Simon Arblinton!' said Marcia. 'He must have heard that Simon was taking time off to join an expedition, and he must have hacked into Simon's emails to check it out. As soon as he read Professor Gadling's earliest emails about Wilfred's find, he'd have realised he'd found what he was looking for.'

'Yes,' said Hal, 'though we didn't know any of that then. We arrived at the temple site two days ago, just as Sebastian was leaving. So we trailed him, always in disguise of course. That night, we caught up with him at the Teluk Batukecil turtle sanctuary in Malaysia, where we saw that he was joining your expedition.'

'We already knew about your expedition,' said Antha. 'Our environmental adviser to the Malaysian government had heard that you'd obtained permission to make a scientific trip to the island. We hoped that you were simply coming here to study the wildlife, as others have done occasionally, but we weren't sure. One of our people who lives in London had a look on board your big flying boat the night before you left the UK, but he could discover nothing.'

'So that's who left the door off its latch,' said Zara, getting a slightly eerie feeling as she remembered her disturbed night on the *Pelican Queen*.

'It was only when we saw Sebastian join your expedition that we made a connection between you and him,' said Peplo. 'And then, of course, we thought that you must all be in on his plans. Staying concealed in the trees some way from the bungalow, we radioed Ushrol and Antha to warn them that Sebastian was on his way here with your expedition.'

'That is when I warned Marno and Embie not to go out,' said Antha. 'But as you saw, in trying not to frighten Embie, I failed to make my warning strong enough to deter her.'

'After we'd done that,' continued Peplo, 'we returned to the turtle sanctuary to see if there was anything more we could learn about your precise plans, or anything we could do to sabotage them. We eavesdropped on your evening meal, but learned nothing. Then we noticed that Sebastian had left his rucksack in the back of the jeep. We were just about to look inside it when Sebastian came round to the car park to get it. He took us by surprise, punching and kicking Ubie and me to the ground. Then he grabbed Hal by the throat, making him cry out in pain, and drew out his flick-knife.'

'You need to understand', said Ubie, 'that as a species we instinctively hide from danger rather than fight it. We avoid violence, which is a good thing; but we lack the bravery of your species, which has probably been our biggest disadvantage. So we had had no plans to attack Sebastian directly when we came to the turtle sanctuary. But when I saw the flick-knife pointing at my brother − the knife that in all probability had killed our father − something flipped inside me.'

'It was the same for me,' said Peplo. 'Raw anger took over from fear − a very rare feeling for us. I sprang to my feet, kicked the knife from his hand, and flew at him in a rage. So did Ubie, and somehow the three of us overpowered him. Then you all came charging round the corner at us, and fear and caution got the better of us once more. As you saw, we let go of him and fled. Your expedition set off as planned in the morning.'

'We watched your two aircraft arrive from the top storey

of this crag tower,' Ushrol told the children, as he continued to work on the radio set. 'All through yesterday, while Embie and Marno slept, Antha and I kept an eye you. We saw you fly up to the lake in your little plane, and saw you disappear into the forest – you can just see the lake from this room's window when there's not so much mist. We watched you return to your big aircraft in the bay, but by then these crags were completely clouding over, and soon we could see nothing. Then a little while later we heard an explosion which, from what Antha told us just now, must have been your small plane being shot down by Sebastian. Some time after that we heard the noise of engines, which must have been Sebastian taking off.'

'Yes,' said Ben, and he quickly filled in all the gaps in their hosts' knowledge about what had happened that evening.

'Meanwhile,' said Hal, 'we had set off from the Malaysian mainland in a small motorboat, to come here and try to sabotage Sebastian's plans and help protect Marno and Embie. We travelled all of yesterday, and all last night, and arrived here half an hour ago. We parked the boat in the sea-cave,' he told Antha, 'and came up through that tunnel.'

'You did well,' Antha told them. She sighed. 'Maybe Ushrol and I should have taken Embie and Marno away from the island as soon as you radioed to warn us Sebastian was coming here. But it seemed safer to stay and remain hidden than to risk a sea voyage where we could easily be seen from a flying boat.' She turned to the children. 'What Ubie said is true. Hiding is what we do in a crisis. We find it hard to take any other kind of action.'

'But what exactly is Sebastian's aim in coming here?' asked Ben. 'Is he trying to capture a member of your species?'

'Yes,' said Hal. 'If he'd been prepared, of course, he could have captured one of us in Genoa when he broke into our loft apartment, but we don't think he knew who or what we were until our father burst in on him. Since reading the journal pages, he has known that if he could find our ancient city he would probably find a group of our species living here, and possibly find information about the locations of other groups around the world. Over time, he's planning to capture as many members of our species as possible.'

'But why?' said Zara. 'Why is he wanting to capture any of you?'

'That is something we found out quite recently,' said Peplo. 'In the course of tracking Sebastian down, we discovered that he has set up a highly confidential medical treatment clinic. He has a laboratory standing by at a secret location and a consortium of clients lined up. These clients, male and female, are all young and all extremely wealthy. Some inherited their wealth; some accumulated theirs in ways they would not like to be made public. They have all made considerable advance payments to Sebastian, which have financed his activities so far. When he delivers them what he has promised, they have each agreed to pay him many millions – a total sum that would make Sebastian one of the richest men on earth.'

'What they will be paying for', said Hal, 'is something that no amount of money has ever previously been able to buy. What Sebastian has promised his clients is that once he gets live specimens of our species into his lab, he will be able to discover the part of our genetic make-up that gives us our long lifespan. He plans to extract samples of these genes from us and, because we are such a similar species to *Homo sapiens*, he believes he will be able to implant this genetic material into his clients – and into himself – slowing their ageing and giving them lifespans as long as ours, lifespans of a hundred and forty years or more. He even believes that once he has understood the genetic processes behind our species' longevity, he will be able to refine and modify the genes before implantation to make lifespans beyond two centuries a possibility.'

'Who can say whether what he plans is possible?' said Antha. 'But now you know what Sebastian wishes to capture us for: to use us as a medical commodity – to exploit our biological make-up to enable him and his rich clients to live to two hundred. We will be imprisoned in his laboratory during use, then killed and discarded when we have served our purpose.'

A shocked silence from the children followed this explanation.

'We'll stop him,' said Ben determinedly.

'We will,' agreed Ushrol. 'We *must*.' He looked up from his work. 'That's the radio sorted. Here, Sam, take the aerial over to the window to give us the best transmission and reception. Zara, you send out the call. The sooner we get your authorities looking for Sebastian, the better. As you say, the plane could be miles away by now.'

'It isn't,' said Sam from the window. 'I can see it. It's moored off the north end of the island.'

35

'*What?*' said Marcia, as they all rushed to the window and looked through the curtain of greenery.

'There,' said Sam, pointing. Now that the mist had cleared, they could see right down the valley between two of the nearby crags, over the lake and down to the island's northern coast. Although that part of the coast was about four miles away, they could all see the unmistakable shape of a white flying boat moored just out from a small rocky inlet.

Sam had already taken his compact binoculars from a trouser pocket and was peering through them. 'It's definitely the *Pelican Queen,*' he said, taking in the three engines and the distinctive double tail fin.

'Do you think Sebastian flew back during the night?' said Marcia. 'With him landing all the way over there, we wouldn't have heard the engines.'

But Zara's brain was coming up with a more obvious solution. 'I'm wondering if he ever flew away from the island at all,' she said slowly. 'What if the engine noise fading wasn't him flying away out to sea, but him flying round

217

the island's northern coast and out of earshot that way?'

'That's a point,' said Marcia. 'We shouldn't have jumped to conclusions.'

Ben was automatically envisaging his mental map of the island, and where the *Pelican Queen*'s new mooring would be on it. Another thought occurred to him. A worrying thought. 'That inlet where the plane's moored,' he said to Antha. 'Isn't that where the river comes out to the sea? The river that flows out from the lake, I mean.'

As Ushrol had said earlier, the lake was just visible from the window, about half a mile to the north of the crag tower they were in. And Ben could glimpse parts of the river, flowing out from the lake's far end and meandering down through the forest.

'Yes,' said Antha, 'the inlet is where the river joins the sea. But why would he have moved the plane round to there?'

'So he could have come up the river to the lake in our inflatable boat!' said Ben. 'He was in a hurry to get to the middle of the island. He was planning to use our little flying boat, but when that plan failed, he had to make a new plan. I bet he came up the river during the night! Our boat's got an outboard motor, but it's almost silent – you'd never have heard it from here, even when he got to the lake.'

Sam used his binoculars again. 'I can't see the inflatable boat on the lake,' he reported. 'But then, I can't see this end of the lake at all, because of the trees. So the boat could be there.'

'It *would* be possible to get up that river in a small boat,' said Antha, 'though difficult in the dark, especially for one of your species. You really think he could have got himself up to the lake during the night?' She looked and sounded anxious.

'It's not good to think he might already be in this part of the island,' said Ushrol, putting an arm round his wife, 'but he doesn't know how to get into the underground city and find us.'

'But he does!' exclaimed Sam, suddenly getting a cold feeling in his stomach. 'He's got a complete moon moth map pendant. That was all he needed for his plan, once Wilfred had shown us where the cave was. Sebastian must have read about how the moon moth map pendants worked in the pages from Radelfi's journal, and he must have hoped that the other half of Wilfred's would be lying buried in the cave somewhere. If you remember, it was just after Zara found it that he sort of suggested we should call it a day and get back to the *Pelican Queen*; he wanted to drug us all and get back to the cave as quickly as possible. With the complete moon moth pendant, he knew he could navigate his way between the cave and the underground city!'

'But Sam,' said Zara, 'you're forgetting that the tunnel system between that cave and the city got blocked up in the earthquake of five thousand years ago. He can't use it – can't even get into it. The back of the cave is totally blocked up with rubble, remember?'

'No,' said Sam. 'Sebastian *told* us it was totally blocked up when he was up on the heap of rubble hanging the lamp. He seemed to be having a good look at something, though. What if he'd seen a narrow way through up there, a way of getting behind the heap of rubble and into the tunnel system? I don't suppose he could be *certain* there was still a way through to the city, but he might have decided to try it anyway. And are we a hundred per cent sure that the middle of that tunnel *did* collapse in the earthquake?'

'Sam's got a point!' said Hal, heading for the room's door. 'If our historians have never rediscovered this tunnel system, because the cave entrance looks blocked and because the city entrance is lost under the ruins, how can we be certain that the middle of the tunnel system isn't still usable? *How can we be certain that Sebastian isn't using it now?*'

Antha was already rushing from the room. 'We should go back down to Marno and Embie,' she said. 'If there's a possibility that Sebastian can get into the city, I think we should leave down the sea-cave tunnel. We could take the boats and—'

BLAM!

An explosion resounded up through the crag tower, emanating from somewhere beneath them – an explosion horribly similar to one the children had heard and felt very recently, as their plane had been crippled by Sebastian's missile.

After a second of stunned shock, there was a scramble for the lift basket. As all ten people piled in, Hal flung the lever forward and the overladen lift went plummeting downwards. An acrid smell of explosives filled the lift shaft, getting stronger as they descended. With a jolt, the basket hit the floor of the alcove. Everyone ran down the winding corridor, into grey smoke and swirling rock dust. Zara knew they could all be running into danger, but no one was thinking of their own safety. They had to get to Embie and Marno.

They reached the part of the passageway near the home's front door – or rather, what had been the front door. All that was left of it were a few charred timbers hanging from one side of the blackened stone door frame, and a scattering of splintered planks. The other side of the door frame and much of the wall around it had been reduced to rubble – rubble that had been blasted several metres along the passageway with the bits of door. Lying beneath a piece of

wood and several blocks of stone, covered in grey dust, was
Marno.

Antha ran to him. Blood was streaming from several
injuries to his face and chest, but he was desperately trying
to prop himself up on his elbows.

'Embie!' he cried, pointing to the gaping, blown-open
front doorway. 'He's taken Embie!'

36

'I was here in the passageway,' stammered Marno shakily. 'Just getting Embie a book from my room . . . Explosion . . . sent me flying. I was out for few seconds . . . Didn't see him come in. But I saw him leave, carrying Embie over shoulder . . . dart in her leg.'

'We'll get him!' uttered Hal, already sprinting out through the wrecked doorway with Ubie and Peplo. 'I promise we'll save Embie!'

'Take care!' Antha cried out after them. 'Remember he's armed!'

'He can shoot us but he won't stop us!' Peplo called back, with reckless determination.

The children sped after the brothers, but Ben and Marcia felt Ushrol's hand grab their elbows, holding them back.

'They might not be able to catch him up,' the old man said, wheezing from the exertion of hobbling at speed, 'especially if he makes it back into the hidden tunnel before they see him. But there's a chance for you two to head him off at the lake – come on!'

Ushrol hurried back towards the lift, and Ben and Marcia, puzzled though they were, hurried with him, helping him along by his arm. Clearly Ushrol had a plan, and any plan had to be worth trying.

Out in the huge cavern, Zara, Sam and Adam raced through the ruined city after Hal, Peplo and Ubie.

'Can you see him?' Zara called.

'No,' said Hal, 'but we're on his trail.'

The three brothers had slowed their pace slightly and were scanning the ground as they ran, which allowed the children to catch them up.

'Dusty footprints, see?' said Peplo, pointing down.

Zara couldn't make out any dusty footprints on the dimly lit grey flagstones. These men were clearly very good at tracking.

They hurried on through the ruins, mostly running but sometimes having to scramble over the ancient masonry.

Suddenly Zara noticed that two of their group were missing. 'Hey,' she said, 'where are Ben and Marcia?'

Ben and Marcia were in the lift with Ushrol, speeding upwards. Ushrol let the lift go past the level they had stopped at last time, and all the way up to the top of the shaft, just below the cables' pulley wheels.

The landing at this highest level was very small, with a tiny slit window.

'Through there,' ordered Ushrol, pointing to a little wooden door as Ben helped him out of the lift. The doorway led into a windowless room, almost as cramped as the landing. The space was cluttered with slightly strange tools, half-finished woodcarvings, unidentifiable bric-a-brac, and what looked to be spare bits of lift machinery. Ushrol dragged an

223

incomplete sculpture of a hornbill away from a corner of the room, and picked up two bulky bundles of black canvas. They looked like rucksacks, except that there were more straps and clips, arranged into harnesses. 'With these', said Ushrol, 'you can glide down to the lake.'

'I think Ushrol kept Ben and Marcia back,' said Adam. 'He needed them for something back there.'

'OK,' said Zara, panting as they kept up with the three brothers.

'Sebastian went down here!' called Hal, who had reached the corner of one of the larger ruined buildings, and was crawling under a fallen pillar. 'See? Here's the stun dart that Marno said was in Embie's leg.'

Zara looked down at the needle-tipped stun dart that Hal had spotted. It looked like the kind she'd seen safari vets use on television. It lay at the edge of a slender, dark gap at the base of the collapsed building. With the toppled pillar concealing it, the gap was barely noticeable. If this was the entrance to the tunnel system, it wasn't surprising that it had never been rediscovered.

One by one, they scrambled through after Hal, but Sam had a thought. 'If two of us ran down the sea-cave tunnel you mentioned and zoomed round the coast in one of your boats,' he said, 'do you think we could get to the *Pelican Queen* first?'

'No,' said Peplo. 'Good idea, but it's a long way down the sea-cave tunnel, and Ushrol's boat is slow and ours needs refuelling. *This* tunnel system can't be as long, and Sebastian will be able to really speed down that river with the current behind him. Our only chance to stop him getting away with Embie is to catch him before he gets to the lake.'

By now they had all got through the gap, and found

themselves on a dark, narrow stairway. Sam and Zara switched their torches on as they rushed down the steps, which led, as expected, to a cave tunnel. They ran along it, but quickly found themselves at a junction where the tunnel split into three. For the first time since beginning the chase, the brothers paused.

'No more footprints,' said Ubie, after they'd checked the ground. 'The dust must've all shaken off by the time he got here. Which way do we try?'

Zara recalled that none of the brothers had even known this tunnel system existed until a few moments ago. How could they possibly find their way?

'We'll have to split up,' said Hal, starting to head down the left–hand tunnel.

'No, wait,' said Peplo. 'You can see there are more junctions a little way down each branch, look, and that will be only the *start* of all the different options. You know what these tunnel systems are like. We could each get completely lost within minutes, without any of us finding the proper route. And even if one of us got lucky, what then? Our only hope of overpowering Sebastian is to attack him together.'

'Only if we can catch up with him,' said Ubie, 'but we can't! Sebastian's got the only moon moth map for this cave system.'

'Actually, I think I've got the map in my head,' announced Adam quietly, in his matter-of-fact way of speaking. He was standing, as he had been for the last few seconds, with his eyes shut and his forehead furrowed in concentration. 'I had a good look at it yesterday when we got back to the *Pelican Queen*, and I can bring the picture of what I saw back into my head. But I don't think I'll be able to hold it there while we're running along. Have you got a notebook and pencil, Sam?'

From his well-equipped pockets, Sam quickly supplied Adam with both items, then held his torch steady while Adam worked. With remarkable speed, Adam first drew a simple outline of the moth wings, omitting all unnecessary details, then filled in the pattern of curving interconnected lines. There was something slightly eerie about his quick, precise hand movements, and something almost trancelike about his torchlit face as he worked. Nobody spoke, or even breathed loudly, for fear of distracting him. Hal, Peplo and Ubie looked absolutely flabbergasted.

'There,' said Adam, after about forty-five seconds. 'I'm sure those are all the lines that were on it.' He handed the notebook to Hal.

'But . . . how could you *do* that?' said Hal. 'Are you *sure* this pattern is identical?'

'Trust him,' said Zara, in an authoritative tone that left no room for doubt.

'OK,' said Hal, wasting no more time on questions. 'You're the quickest map-reader, Peplo,' he said, handing the map to his brother.

'We're here,' said Peplo, pointing to the junction of lines nearest to the pattern right edge. 'The city entrance to a tunnel system is always placed on the right-hand side of a map pendant. And we need to take the middle tunnel at this junction. Let's go.'

'Well done, Adam,' said Zara, squeezing Adam's hand as they set off after the brothers. She noticed that his mental exertions had left him looking drained.

The six of them half-jogged and half-clambered through the tunnels. Knowing that their best weapon against Sebastian was surprise, they avoided talking and kept their footsteps as quiet as possible. Zara turned her torch off, while Sam cupped his in his fingers, keeping it pointed down

rather than letting it shine ahead. The brothers continued
to lead the way, using only their tiny dim collar lamps.

Their progress was swift. Hal's ability to read the small,
complex map without pausing at any of the junctions was
almost as remarkable as Adam's feats of photographic memory and speed-drawing. Zara was sure that Sebastian
wouldn't be able to navigate his way through the tunnels so
quickly, and became hopeful that they might catch up with
him before he reached the exit at the skeleton cave. But her
hope was mixed with fear. They were pursuing a ruthless
killer, whom they knew to be armed with a missile-
launcher and other weaponry, along a confined space, with
no plan of how they were going to tackle him if they did
catch him up. It seemed madness, but there had been no
other option. If Sebastian escaped, Zara was certain that
neither Embie, nor the adults on the *Pelican Queen*, would
ever be seen again.

37

'Basically, they're hang-gliders,' said Ushrol, hurriedly strapping Ben into the harness of the bulky bag. 'Collapsible hang-gliders of my own unique design. I have always been interested in gliding, inspired no doubt by watching the many gliding creatures of this island. And I constructed this second hang-glider to teach some of the visitors we have had over the years. I have only glided at night, of course, when I could be sure no one out at sea would notice me. I *would* pilot one of the hang-gliders now, except I am too old and frail to be of much use on the ground. So I am relying on you two.' He finished fastening the straps and sorted Marcia's harness out. Neither Ben nor Marcia felt at all sure about this idea, but Ushrol was already hustling them up a ladder, which led to a round stone hatch in the ceiling.

'Up you go,' he insisted, coming up after them. 'Push the hatch open . . . It's too heavy for me these days . . . That's it, go through. I'm right behind you.'

Ben found himself emerging onto the very top of the crag – a slightly sloping rectangle of rock less than two metres wide. With Marcia coming up behind him, Ben had to move away from the hatchway. He crawled across the crag-top gingerly, then sat down. Marcia followed, to make room for Ushrol. Neither of them dared to stand up. The bird's-eye, panoramic view of the island was stupendous, but absolutely terrifying.

'Look, we've never flown anything like hang-gliders before,' said Marcia.

'If you can fly a plane, you can fly my hang-glider,' said Ushrol, kneeling beside them. 'That's why I picked you two. Trust me – it's easy. Your flying position's much like that of an ordinary hang-glider pilot: head forward, legs trailing out the back. But the wing's like a paraglider wing – made from tubes of fabric that fill with air as it moves forward, to give it its shape. And I designed it to open out from the backpack after jumping, like a parachute, so that I could launch myself from a place with limited space, like this. It's simple. Now, I'll talk you through the controls.'

Ushrol quickly showed them the toggle that deployed the fabric wing, the strap that reduced the wing area in order to lose height, and the lines that controlled steering. Ben wasn't sure he was taking any of it in properly. His stomach felt leaden and his mind was replaying the horrible moment when he had been wrestling in vain with the controls of the *Silver Turtle*, totally powerless to stop them all plummeting to their deaths. He was sure he'd lost his nerve for flying, and he was sure he simply wasn't capable of launching himself off this horrendously high crag with nothing but a bag of fabric strapped to his back. He glanced at Marcia and suspected she was having similar thoughts.

'Your safest landing place is in the lake itself,' said Ushrol, apparently oblivious to his pilots' concerns. He handed them a pair of small sharp chisels that he'd brought up from the room below them. 'Find the boat and sabotage it with these,' he said. 'Burst the sides and wreck the motor. If you can stop Sebastian using the river, he's got a long trek, and the others will be able to catch him up or beat him to the flying boat. Good luck. And thank you. You go first, Ben.'

Ben put his chisel in one of his trouser pockets and made himself shuffle forwards until his legs were hanging over the edge. The drop looked even worse. He was sure he couldn't do this. But he had to. He couldn't let Ushrol down. Couldn't let Embie down. Couldn't let the adults in the *Pelican Queen* down. Without giving himself time to think any more about it, he put the soles of his feet against the side of the crag, leaned forward, and gave a kick with both legs, pushing himself out into thin air.

As soon as he was clear of the crag, he pulled the toggle. After a terrifying plummet that seemed to last for several seconds (but which actually lasted for only one) he felt and heard something arrest his descent with a jolting whump.

And then he was gliding – gliding smoothly over the forested hill valley. Almost unable to believe it had worked, he looked

up. Fixed to his backpack by four thin lines was a large, black fabric wing, its tubed surface filling with air to form a curved airfoil, just as Ushrol had said it would.

Looking up had shifted his

weight, and he realised he was veering dangerously close to one of the other crags. What had Ushrol said about steering? Pull the control line. Just a bit ... Not too much. That was it. Back on course. He was getting the hang of it now, sailing between the crags, with the treetops flashing past way beneath him. From somewhere behind him, he heard the old man calling, 'Well done, both of you!'

He glanced back and saw, with relief, that Marcia's hang-glider was flying fine as well, a little way behind him and a little lower. Marcia's face was fixed in concentration as she piloted a steadily descending course. It occurred to Ben that he, however, was actually getting higher. The warm air rising up from the forest was lifting him towards the level of the crag-tops.

For a moment, he considered attempting to fly as far as the *Pelican Queen*, where he would be able to remove Sebastian's means of escape permanently, and from where he could email or radio for help. But, as a minor error in his piloting sent the hang-glider lurching slightly, his sense of caution returned. As he corrected the error, he realised that he could all too easily crash into the rainforest between here and the inlet on the northern coast, and then he would be of no help to anybody. Stick to plan A, he decided. He pulled on the control strap which reduced the wing area. As the hang-glider began to lose height, he managed to hold a more or less steady course towards the lake.

Remembering Amy's method of approach, he came over the lakeside trees as low as he could, then quickly lost even more height. The manoeuvre sent him splashing down into the water in the centre of the lake. The landing lacked elegance, but had got him down uninjured and in the right place.

His head buzzing with relief and adrenalin, he detached

himself from his harness, duck-dived clear of the tangle of lines and fabric that were floating down on top of him, and surfaced just in time to see Marcia make her landing. She splashed down nearer to the shingly shore than he had, and gave a cry of pain as she did so.

'Are you all right?' called Ben anxiously, swimming over to her.

'Banged my knee on a rock,' Marcia said, wincing. 'Landed too shallow. I'm all right though.'

Ben helped her disentangle herself from her lines and canvas, and lent her an arm as they waded to the shore.

'Can you see the boat?' asked Marcia, scanning the lakeside.

'No,' said Ben, worried and puzzled. They reached the shingle beach, where Marcia had to sit down. Ben stepped up onto one of the big, flat rocks to get a better view of the whole shoreline. But there was no sign of the boat anywhere.

'Do you think Sebastian could have got back here before we started gliding?' asked Marcia. 'And already be heading down the river?'

'No,' said Ben, after a moment's thought. 'He couldn't possibly have got through the cave tunnel more quickly than we got to the top of the crag tower. But what if our whole idea about Sebastian using the boat was wrong?'

'It can't be,' countered Marcia. 'How else could he have got from the *Pelican Queen* to the skeleton cave by this morning if he didn't come up the river?' She thought some more, and the most likely answer came to her. 'He must have hidden the boat before going to the cave,' she said, struggling back onto her feet. 'He would have wanted to make sure that it wasn't discovered while he was gone. Come on – the plants up there at the back of this beach are the most likely place.'

With Marcia hobbling up the shingle behind him, insisting her knee was all right and that he should go on ahead, Ben began to hurriedly scour the jungly vegetation that fringed the lakeside shingle.

38

Peplo, who was leading them single file through a narrow stretch of tunnel, suddenly stopped. He held up his hand to the others, clearly indicating that absolute silence was required. Everyone listened and heard what Peplo had heard: the sound of someone walking over loose stones, not far ahead of them – just around the next curve of the tunnel from the sound of it.

The three brothers glanced at each other and nodded. Hal signalled to the children that they should stay behind them, and that Sam should switch off his torch.

At first it seemed to Sam that it was too dark to see at all. But as his eyes adjusted, he found that the brothers' collar lamps were emitting just enough of a faint glow to enable him vaguely to make out the tunnel walls as they crept forward. But the children were mostly relying on their hands rather than their eyes to negotiate their way through the rocky passage. Sam's heart was pounding and his hands were trembling. They were about to catch up with a man who was armed and dangerous. They could all lose their lives.

As they rounded the corner, the tunnel suddenly widened into a bigger space. The space was very dark, but not quite as dark as the tunnel behind them. About fifteen metres ahead and several metres up, everyone could make out a faint grey patch of diffused daylight – a narrow gap at the top of a heap of rocks and boulders that were otherwise blocking the way completely. Clearly, this was the other side of the heap of rocks that blocked off the back of the skeleton cave.

In the dark-grey gloom, the figure of Sebastian could just be seen starting to clamber up the boulder heap, with Embie slung unconscious over his left shoulder. There was no light from any torch, though it occurred to Sam that Sebastian must surely have used one earlier when coming through the tunnels, and he wondered why he'd switched it off now.

Sebastian was obviously unaware of their presence in the shadows behind him. Hal, Peplo and Ubie gave clear hand signals that the children were to wait here, then switched off their collar lamps. As the brothers began to move forward silently, and almost invisibly in the darkness, Zara appreciated that these people's extraordinary agility and eyesight were their best weapon against Sebastian. Much as she wanted to do something to help, she knew that she, Sam and Adam would merely alert Sebastian if they moved forward too. So the three children hung back, ready to pitch in as soon as the brothers grabbed Sebastian, as soon as the element of surprise became redundant.

But before the brothers had covered half the distance to the foot of the boulder heap, Hal's foot kicked a tiny stone. Sebastian spun round at the noise, grabbed a pistol-like weapon from his belt and aimed it. *Ffft. Ffft. Ffft.* Even though it was dark, and even though the three brothers had fanned out to make their assault, two of Sebastian's shots hit their mark, sending Peplo and Ubie dropping to the floor. Stun darts, Zara guessed. He wanted more live specimens to come back for. She was already racing forward to help

Hal, with Sam and Adam beside her.

Hal dived at Sebastian and the two of them rolled onto the floor, sending Embie falling from Sebastian's shoulder.

As Sam charged into the fray he could just make out that Sebastian had something dark and bulky over his eyes. Night-vision goggles! That was how he'd seen without a torch.

Ffft. Just as Zara flung herself at Sebastian, he managed to get a close shot into Hal's leg. Hal collapsed instantly, and Sebastian was back on his feet. Zara and Adam grabbed the dart gun and tried to grapple it from his grasp.

'You!' exclaimed Sebastian, clearly astonished that they had survived the crash of the *Silver Turtle* and were now here.

They almost prised the dart gun from him, but with his left hand, Sebastian pulled another weapon from his belt – they couldn't see what in the dark – and pointed it at Zara's chest. Just as he pulled the trigger, Sam cannoned into him, sending him onto his back once more and causing the weapon to point upwards.

Whoooosssssshhhhh!

There was no doubt now what the weapon was. A small sleek missile came scooshing out of its wide, tubular barrel and rocketed straight up, streaming a trail of white-hot fire behind it that illuminated the whole cavernous space.

BLAM!

The missile exploded on impact with the craggy ceiling, high above them, filling the upper part of the cave with a mushrooming ball of fire, as the deafeningly loud noise reverberated through the confined space.

Ben and Marcia had been searching for several minutes when Marcia spotted the boat. It had been slid beneath some thick bushes at the side of the river, just downstream from the lake.

'It's here!' she called to Ben, who was still working his way through the bushes at the back of the shingle beach.

Ben ran to join Marcia, quickly catching her up as she was still limping from her knee injury. But as they approached the concealed boat, chisels in hand, they heard a muffled explosion.

They span round. The sound had come from the forest – from the direction of the cave.

'Sebastian's missile-launcher!' exclaimed Marcia. She felt suddenly sick with dread. If he'd fired another missile, the target had to be the people who were pursuing him.

The same awful thought sprang into Ben's mind. 'Come on,' he yelled, racing back along the lakeside and plunging into the forest, taking the jungle path they had cut the day before. Whether Marcia was limping after him or staying to deal with the boat, he wasn't sure. But he had to get to the cave, had to help the others if he could. If it wasn't too late.

Sebastian, already seeming stunned by his backwards fall, put his hands to his night-vision goggles, shielding his eyes from the brightness of the explosion above. Zara sprang to her feet, trying to think clearly. She became aware that dust, small bits of rock and broken stalactites were starting to fall from above, and that the whole ceiling was making strange graunching noises.

'*The ceiling's about to collapse!*' she yelled to Sam and Adam. 'Try to drag Hal and the other two back into the tunnel! I'll get Embie! *Run!*'

She rushed to scoop up Embie, who was still unconscious, flung her over her shoulder and ran for the tunnel. Through the swirling smoke of the explosion, she could see Sam and Adam ahead of her, dragging Hal between them by his arms. Zara almost tripped over the motionless body of Peplo. Without stopping, and still carrying Embie, she reached down and dragged him along with her by his collar.

The erratic shower of stones from above was increasing in intensity, and the ominous noises were growing louder. Zara was sure that the whole ceiling was going to go at any second. Ahead of her, she could see that Sam and Adam had got Hal to the tunnel, and were coming back for Ubie, who had been brought down nearest to its entrance. '*Quick!*' she yelled as they dragged him to safety, too. She was almost at the tunnel herself. Almost safe.

BANG! BANG! BANG!

Three shots rang out behind her from yet another weapon – Sebastian's automatic – and she felt a sudden pain in her left calf. As her leg gave way, she fell sideways, dropping Embie near her.

Out of the corner of her eye, Zara saw Sebastian's hand seize Embie's ankle and yank her up from the floor.

Zara turned and tried to get up but couldn't, tried to make a grab for Embie's trailing arms. But Sebastian was away. Helplessly, through the veil of falling stones, Zara watched him pelt across the space with Embie over his shoulder once more, watched him scrabble with desperate speed up the heap of boulders.

'You should have stayed out of this!' he shouted back to

Zara and the others, as he disappeared through the pale grey gap at the top. 'These apes were no concern of yours.'

He was just through, just out of sight, when the shower of stones became a sudden torrent. Zara felt Sam and Adam's hands dragging her to safety, just in time, as the ceiling came crashing down.

Ben sprinted uphill through the rainforest. As he drew near to the bank of rock, he could see clouds of dust spewing from the cave and inside, a shower of stones tumbling down – tumbling down on the small motionless figure of Embie. Without slowing, Ben charged into the cave. Ignoring the stones hitting his head, he scooped Embie up, then darted back towards safety. But bigger rocks were falling now. A boulder struck him on the shoulder, knocking him down. As he fell forward onto his chest, he managed to fling Embie out through the cave-mouth. But he hit the cave floor some way short of it. For a second or two, he had a view of the outside world, green and out of reach. Then, as a cascade of heavy boulders and rocks rained down on him, everything went black.

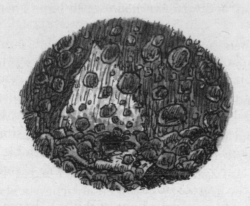

39

When Ben recovered consciousness, he found he was lying on his back in a bed. His sides hurt, and so did his left arm and his right leg. Opening his eyes fully, he attempted to sit up, but stopped immediately. When he moved, the pain in his limbs and ribs became much worse. His head was throbbing painfully, too.

'Don't try to move too much,' said a gravelly voice.

Ben turned his head and saw that Ushrol was sitting on a chair beside the bed. And there were most of the others, standing in a group behind him: Antha, Embie, Hal, Sam, Marcia and Adam.

'You're awake!' cried Zara's voice from somewhere, as Marcia, Sam and Adam rushed over to him. 'Thank goodness!'

The others crowded round, too, though Ushrol warned them not to jolt the patient. Ben saw that he was in a room similar to Embie's, and then he saw Marno, half-sitting up in a hammock on the other side of the room with bandages round his chest. The boy's face was badly scarred and bruised, but its previous expression of hostility was gone, replaced by a smile.

Where was Zara? There – on another bed at the foot of his, sitting up and looking immensely relieved. Her left calf was bandaged.

'What happened to you?' Ben asked her, finding his face hurt when he spoke. He wondered if it was as bruised as Marno's. 'And have I broken anything?'

'Your left arm is fractured, and I think you have cracked a rib,' said Ushrol. 'I have bandaged your arm with a splint, and also bandaged your ribcage. Your right leg is badly bruised but not broken, and the same goes for your head – no skull fractures. You were lucky. So was Zara. A bullet in her calf muscle, but easily extracted. It will heal.'

Ben found that his woozy brain could remember hearing the explosion and then running to the cave, but not much else. 'What exactly happened?' he asked. And how long have I been unconscious?'

'You've been out for about six hours,' said Zara. 'We were really worried.'

'Sebastian fired another missile,' said Sam, answering Ben's first question, 'and it caused another rockfall – a huge one. The whole roof of the cave collapsed. We were on the other side of the boulders, and got back into the tunnels – just.'

'They got me and my brothers back into the tunnels, too,' said Hal. 'We'd be dead otherwise. Sebastian had stundarted us.'

'After the rocks stopped falling,' said Sam, 'we saw that the collapsed ceiling had left a new way through to the skeleton cave. I stayed with Zara, to bandage her leg with a torn shirt, while Adam climbed through. We had to find out what had happened to Embie. Sebastian had been carrying her, and we knew he'd been right at the top of the boulder heap when the rockfall happened.'

'As I was climbing through, we heard Marcia calling,' said Adam.

'With my knee slowing me down, I got to the cave after

the rockfall had stopped,' said Marcia. 'I found Embie lying just outside the mouth of the cave. Then I saw you, Ben, lying just inside, covered in rocks. I only spotted you because one of your hands was sticking out.'

Marcia shuddered as her mind replayed the moment when they'd found Ben, the terrible moment when she thought that he'd met the same fate as the skeleton whose hand Wilfred had spotted fifty years ago.

'Did you throw Embie out of the cave, before the rocks came down on you?' asked Adam. 'We couldn't see how she could have got there otherwise.'

Ben nodded. His memory of what had happened was coming back now. 'I got to the cave just in time to spot her.'

'You saved my life,' said Embie. 'Thank you.'

'And nearly lost your life doing it,' added Marno. 'You all did. Thank you. And sorry. Sorry for thinking that people of your species would never care about people like us.'

'Any time,' said Ben, not knowing what else to say. 'What happened to Sebastian?'

'Dead,' said Antha. 'After they'd found you and Embie, Adam and Sam ran back through the tunnels to fetch me. By the time I got here, Embie had woken up, and Hal, Peplo and Ubie were beginning to come round. Once we had got you and Zara back up here for medical attention, and once the boys were strong enough, we searched through the rubble and found Sebastian. He must have died quickly. His head had been badly crushed.' There was no malice or triumphalism in her voice. 'A pointless end to a badly lived life,' she said.

'We have given him a proper burial,' Ushrol told Ben.

'He never regarded us as humans, but that is no reason for us to stop behaving like humans.'

'And what about the adults?' said Ben anxiously. 'Did you find them on the *Pelican Queen*. They are all right, aren't they?'

'Yes,' said Sam. 'They're all fine. Some of us went down the tunnel system that leads to the sea-cave, and drove round the coast to the *Pelican Queen* in one of the motor-boats. We found the adults all handcuffed to the chairs in the lounge, still unconscious but otherwise fine, as far as we could tell. We towed the *Pelican Queen* back round the coast, and we've moored her near the sea-cave. Hal zoomed back here to get the handcuff key from one of Sebastian's pockets so that we could release the adults and put them into their bunks. Peplo and Ubie have stayed down there to keep an eye on them. If what Sebastian told us was true about the sleeping drug wearing off after thirty-six hours, the adults should wake up first thing tomorrow morning.'

'I can see we are going to have to let *them* know about us, too,' said Antha. 'But after all you have done for us, I feel confident that any friends of yours are likely to be people we can trust.'

At dawn the next day, everyone except Ben, Zara and Marno (who needed to remain resting) and Ushrol and Hal (who stayed to look after them) was on board the *Pelican Queen*.

Sam, Adam and Marcia (whose knee was almost back to normal), spread themselves between the adult's three cabins. They watched with great relief as the six adults – Amy, Gabrielle, Wilfred, and Professors Gadling, Gauntraker and Ampersand – began to wake up. They were all pretty drowsy at first, but were soon on their feet and demanding to know why none of them could remember going to bed, and why they had been sleeping in their clothes. Marcia gathered them in the corridor and, before taking them through to the lounge, she explained that Simon had not been Simon at all, and that he had drugged them. They were all deeply shocked.

'We'll tell you who he really was in a minute,' said Marcia, 'and how we escaped from him. Don't worry – we're all OK. But first we need to introduce you to some people who've been helping us. This is going to be an even bigger shock – but a good one.'

She led them through to the lounge, where Antha, Embie, Peplo and Ubie were waiting. For several seconds, the six adults stood speechless with absolute astonishment.

Wilfred was the first to speak. 'You . . . you're not extinct!' he blurted out. 'You're still living here! This is . . . this is . . . this is fantastic!'

'Good lord!' said Professor Gauntraker solemnly. 'In all my years of exploring, I have never encountered anything as extraordinary, anything as marvellous as this. Do you . . . er . . . speak English?'

'We do,' said Antha, giving a slight bow of greeting with her head.

'We . . . we're pleased tae meet you,' said Amy in a dazed voice, holding out her hand to shake theirs.

'Oh . . . er . . . absolutely,' said Professor Ampersand, doing the same. 'Marcia tells me you've been helping them. Many thanks.'

Professor Gadling opened his mouth to speak. 'How . . .' he began. 'That is to say, where . . . I mean, what . . . How . . .' His attempts at a sentence petered out. For once, Professor Garrulous Gadling was absolutely lost for words.

'I think', croaked Gabrielle, 'that what we need ter do is ter make a massive pot of strong tea, sit down, and have someone explain this entire thing to us properly.'

It was decided to follow this suggestion and soon, as they all sat drinking tea, the three children related all the recent events. This took some time, but at last, all the adults were fully acquainted with the facts. Then Antha, after swearing them to secrecy, told the adults the whole story of her species, as she had told it to the children the day before.

'Well,' said Professor Gadling, finding his power of speech once more, 'I've always said that the world contains more mysteries than we can imagine, but not even I believed it contained a secret as unimaginably extraordinary as this! And to think that those narrow-minded old snobs at the Royal Westminster Institute of Natural History told Wilfred he hadn't found anything even worth looking at. I'd like to wipe that condescending look off their president's face by walking into his office with one of our new friends here and . . . I realise we can't, of course,' he added quickly. 'But it's a shame you'll never be able to prove to them how wrong they were, Wilfred.'

'I don't care about them now,' said Wilfred. 'I don't care about proving anything to anyone. Finding out that these people are still living and getting to meet them is better than anything I could have dreamt of – far, far better than making my name for discovering a five-thousand-year-old skeleton.'

Over the next few days, Ben, Zara and Marno began to make good recoveries. Their injuries would need to be bandaged for a while, and would take some time to heal fully, but soon all three of them were able to get out of their beds and go outside. For the first few days they used makeshift wheelchairs that Ushrol, Sam and Professor Ampersand built in Ushrol's workshop. After that, they could manage with walking sticks. Embie and Marno showed the five *Homo sapiens* children all their favourite places on the island.

Hal, Ubie and Peplo took all their visitors on a few night-time nature walks through the rainforest. Marcia and the others found it a much less scary place at night when accompanied by guides who could see in the dark, and they saw all kinds of amazing nocturnal creatures, including more of the island's black moon moths.

During the days, the three brothers helped to salvage some parts of the *Silver Turtle* from its crash site. Amy had been philosophical when she learned that the little plane she had spent so long designing and building had been wrecked. The main thing, she said, was that no one had been killed, and she congratulated Marcia for her emergency crash landing in the tree canopy. She and Professor Ampersand supervised the salvage operation, and the agile brothers managed to recover many valuable parts — cockpit instruments, motor components, the energy cells, wheels, and suchlike. These were carried through the forest to the bay and stowed in the *Pelican Queen*'s hold, so that they could be taken home and used in the replacement aircraft that Amy and Professor Ampersand were already planning to build.

After some thought, Antha and Ushrol decided that Professor Sharpe, Professor Hartleigh-Broadbeam and Sam's parents should be told the secret of their species' existence, once the expedition had returned to the UK. (No one wanted to risk sending such sensitive information by email, after what had happened before.) A big factor in their decision was the other professors' hope that Professor Sharpe might be able to use her connections to arrange some secret medical help for tackling the devastating illness that Antha had told them about.

It was while this discussion was being conducted, over breakfast in the tower crag, that Zara decided to raise something with Antha that she'd been mulling over in her mind for some time.

'Do you not sometimes think that you'd be better off if

you didn't keep yourself secret from our species at all?' she asked, tentatively. 'I mean, the reason why Sebastian was able to get away with killing Azlo was because Hal, Peplo and Ubie couldn't go to the police. And the reason he would have been able to carry out his plans to capture Embie and the rest of you and keep you in his laboratory was because no one would report you missing.'

'She's got a point,' said Professor Ampersand. 'If our species knew about you, you'd have the same legal protections as all humans.'

'Maybe,' said Antha. 'Or the same chance of being bombed to pieces as all humans. Some members of my species believe the time may be near when we should trust your species, but others are not so sure, and whenever members of your species start a new round of warfare or environmental destruction, their argument for having nothing to do with you is strengthened.'

'I'm sorry,' said Marcia. 'Our species is ruining the planet for everyone else on it.'

'Don't be *too* hard on your species,' said Antha. 'Your species has progressed such a long way, has achieved so much, and is capable of such great things, as we've all seen from you and your friends. None of the challenges that your species faces will be made easier if you start hating yourselves. Maybe one day, your species will become fully civilised, and ready to share the planet with us. Maybe one day we will come out of hiding.'

Finally, the morning came when Professor Gauntraker thought they had better be heading for home. They didn't want to get caught by the winter monsoon storm season, and in any case, they were scheduled to be back in the UK in five days' time.

Wilfred had an announcement to make. He had decided to stay on the island. 'I've nothing to go back to in London,' he said. 'And throughout my life I've never really felt I *belonged*, like I do here. So Antha and Ushrol have said I can live out the rest of my days on the island. I'll be able to make my own myself useful. And they'll be able to send me off on jobs and errands from time to time, when having someone who can move about more easily among our species is an advantage. And I can act as a sort of point of contact between you lot and them in the future.'

Everyone made their fond farewells and thanks. The expedition party took their places aboard the *Pelican Queen*, and Gabrielle started the engines. As the big flying boat taxied round to face the open sea, the children waved through the lounge windows at their hosts and Wilfred, who were standing on the sandy beach, waving back.

The *Pelican Queen* sped across the water and took off into the west to begin the long journey home. Sam clambered along to the very back of the plane, to sit in the glazed observation bubble between the tail fins. He took in his last look at the island, a last look at its verdant landscape and its towering dragon's-teeth crags. With his binoculars, he checked the beach, to see if anyone was still there, waving. But there was no one. For now at least, the people of the island had disappeared back into the shadows of the forest.